Acting Edition

I0584853

Ken Ludwig's

Lend Me a Soprano

‖SAMUEL FRENCH‖

FOR PRODUCTION INQUIRIES

UNITED STATES AND CANADA
info@concordtheatricals.com
1-866-979-0447

UNITED KINGDOM AND EUROPE
licensing@concordtheatricals.co.uk
020-7054-7298

Each title is subject to availability from Concord Theatricals Corp., depending upon country of performance. Please be aware that *LEND ME A SOPRANO* may not be licensed by Concord Theatricals Corp. in your territory. Professional and amateur producers should contact the nearest Concord Theatricals Corp. office or licensing partner to verify availability.

This work is published by Samuel French, an imprint of Concord Theatricals Corp.

No one shall make any changes in this title(s) for the purpose of production. No part of this book may be reproduced, stored in a retrieval system, scanned, uploaded, or transmitted in any form, by any means, now known or yet to be invented, including mechanical, electronic, digital, photocopying, recording, videotaping, or otherwise, without the prior written permission of the publisher. No one shall share this title(s), or any part of this title(s), through any social media or file hosting websites.

For all inquiries regarding motion picture, television, online/digital and other media rights, please contact Concord Theatricals Corp.

MUSIC AND THIRD-PARTY MATERIALS USE NOTE

Licensees are solely responsible for obtaining formal written permission from copyright owners to use copyrighted music and/or other copyrighted third-party materials (e.g. artworks, logos) in the performance of this play and are strongly cautioned to do so. If no such permission is obtained by the licensee, then the licensee must use only original music and materials that the licensee owns and controls. Licensees are solely responsible and liable for clearances of all third-party copyrighted materials, including without limitation music, and shall indemnify the copyright owners of the play(s) and their licensing agent, Concord Theatricals Corp., against any costs, expenses, losses and liabilities arising from the use of such copyrighted third-party materials by licensees. For music, please contact the appropriate music licensing authority in your territory for the rights to any incidental music.

IMPORTANT BILLING AND CREDIT REQUIREMENTS

If you have obtained performance rights to this title, please refer to your licensing agreement for important billing and credit requirements.

LEND ME A SOPRANO was first produced by the Alley Theatre (Rob Melrose, Artistic Director; Dean R. Gladden, Managing Director) in Houston, TX, on September 21, 2022. The performance was directed by Eleanor Holdridge with sets by Klara Zieglerova, costumes by Helen Huang, lighting design by Jorge Arroyo, and sound design by Jane Shaw. The Production Stage Manager was Rachel Dooley-Harris. The cast was as follows:

MRS. WYLIE	Ellen Harvey
JO	Mia Pinero
JERRY	Brandon Hearnsberger
ELENA FIRENZI	Alexandra Silber
PASQUALE	Orlando Arriaga
BELLHOP	Skyler Sinclair
LEO	Steven Good
JULIA	Susan Koozin

CHARACTERS

5 women, 3 men

MRS. WYLIE – General Manager of the Cleveland Grand Opera Company
JO – her assistant
JERRY – her son
ELENA FIRENZI – a world-famous soprano
PASQUALE – Elena's husband
BELLHOP – Beverly, a bellhop
LEO – a tenor
JULIA – Chairwoman of the Opera Guild

The role of the Bellhop was written to be played by a woman, but is not gender-specific. Theatres wishing to change the gender of the Bellhop should change pronouns throughout, as well as the name on page 68.

SETTING

An elegant suite in a first-rate hotel in Cleveland, Ohio.

TIME

September 1934.

NOTE ON MUSIC

Optional performance tracks by Jane Shaw for the below four songs are available for an additional fee. Please contact your licensing representative for more information.

"O mio babbino caro"
"Largo al factotum"
"L'amo come il fulgor del creato"
"O del mio dolce ardor"

AUTHOR'S NOTE

The history of drama over the last 2,000 years is decidedly male-centric. Take, for example, the comedies of William Shakespeare, which I adore. Even though the female characters are now played by women – unlike in Shakespeare's time – the bulk of the parts are still roles for men: Bottom and the other Rude Mechanicals in *A Midsummer Night's Dream*; the many joyful clowns from Costard in *Love's Labour's Lost* to Dogberry in *Much Ado About Nothing*; the whole great host of sons, suitors, servants, and sailors in *Twelfth Night, As You Like It,* and *The Comedy of Errors*. Poor Miranda is literally the only woman in *The Tempest*.

Over the course of my career in professional theatre, I have been continually dazzled by the talent of the women I've worked with, women who deserve a greater share of the juicy roles we love to see brought to life on stage. In my own small way, I've worked to redress the balance by writing more roles for women into my plays. When I adapted Dumas' *The Three Musketeers*, I invented a swashbuckling sister for D'Artagnan. In Sherwood, I created the clever heroine Doerwynn to join Robin Hood's band of Merry Men. But I knew I could do more.

My first Broadway and West End play, *Lend Me A Tenor*, is still one of my most frequently produced. It's the kind of play that is closest to my heart: a boisterously funny one-set comedy for a cast of eight. The cast is evenly split along gender lines, but the three whopping great roles are for men: Max, the timid, would-be opera singer who finds his voice and his confidence over the course of the show; Saunders, Max's boss at the Cleveland Grand Opera who storms his way through the play with volcanic comic aplomb; and Tito, the exuberant, larger-than-life Italian tenor. What would happen, I wondered, if these characters were women? The prospect of re-writing my play so these roles could be brought to life by extraordinary comic actresses took root and *Lend Me A Soprano* was born.

As I started to write the play, I thought I might be able to just turn it on its head – keep most of the dialogue and simply change the names of the characters. Max became Jo, a harried and slightly mousy young woman with aspirations of opera stardom. Saunders became Mrs. Wiley, a tough-as-nails businesswoman holding her own as head of the Cleveland Grand Opera. And Tito Merelli became Elena Firenzi, a tempestuous soprano who sweeps in and turns the world upside down. But it wasn't enough to just change the characters' names and genders. Men and women do not have the same syntax, and they approach challenges with a different lived experience. My project became one of finding the honesty of these women's stories without dulling the comedy or losing sight of the fact that these characters should be just as fun and funny as their male counterparts are in *Tenor*.

Finding the right vocabulary to tell these women's stories meant working closely with talented women who brought their own experiences to the play as it took shape. Being a playwright can be a solitary life, but only a fool refuses to listen to brilliant people who bring their own expertise to the table I was lucky to have brilliant women at the table for the world premiere of *Lend Me A Soprano*, and the play became richer and warmer because of them.

It was clear from the start that the first production of *Soprano* should be directed by a woman, and Eleanor Holdridge was the perfect choice. She and I worked closely to identify those moments in the play where the change in genders undermined the integrity of the story. In particular, some of the sexual antics that are pure comedy in *Tenor* felt uncomfortable in *Soprano*. In *Lend Me A Tenor*, the women seduce the men, so a simple change in genders meant the men in *Lend Me A Soprano* became sexual aggressors. I wanted to ensure that the women still had the agency in this play, just as they do in *Lend Me A Tenor*, and that meant rewriting several scenes.

Changing the women's roles in *Lend Me A Tenor* to men's roles in *Lend Me A Soprano* took special care. For example, in the opening scene of *Lend Me A Tenor*, Max's girlfriend Maggie talks about her desire for excitement and some sexual experience before settling into marriage with her sweet but unexciting boyfriend, which feels unobjectionable. But when I swapped the genders and had Jo's boyfriend Jerry talk about the same desire, he seemed like a creep. I wanted him to sound tender rather than lecherous. He needed to be someone we rooted for, so I wrote a new scene for Jerry to describe the moment when he first met Elena Firenzi backstage after a performance and developed a crush on her.

Likewise, I looked carefully at the character of Leo, formerly the seductive blonde bombshell Diana in *Lend Me A Tenor*. When I changed the character's gender, I decided to make him foreign and lively rather than an ambitious local singer. If I'd kept the dialogue as it was from *Tenor*, he would have seemed debauched. But when I made him into a greater innocent, in love with himself and with being young, and in love with jumping into bed with fellow opera singers for their joy as much as his own, he became honest and just who he was.

I was also lucky to have three incredibly talented comic actresses in the lead roles for the play's premiere. Mia Pinero as Jo, Ellen Harvey as Mrs. Wiley, and Alexandra Silber as Elena Firenzi brought a depth to their characters that I worked to reflect in the script. They drew on their own experiences of being women in theatre, being mentored by other women with long-established careers. They spoke passionately about the importance of nurturing emerging talent, especially women uplifting other women in male-dominated spaces, like professional theatre. They inspired me to enrich the play with themes of mentorship and genuine friendship. It became about Mrs. Wiley cheering Jo on: rather than feeling threatened by her, she takes pride in Jo's development into a confident woman, ready to conquer the world. And it became about a jaded Elena rediscovering her love of art by encouraging Jo's passion for opera and hope for the future.

I returned to the story of *Lend Me A Tenor* because I loved the characters – the same reason I wrote *A Comedy of Tenors*, in which many of them return for another madcap adventure. But *Lend Me A Soprano* became more than just the joy of revisiting these people in their antic world. I think this play is at least as funny as *Lend Me A Tenor* – it has all of *Tenor*'s comic strengths – but I think it also has more warmth and heart. And I feel privileged that so many wonderful women of the theatre will have the opportunity to bring these characters to life.

ACT ONE

Scene One

(An elegant suite in a first-rate hotel in Cleveland, Ohio. Early afternoon on a Saturday in September, 1934.)

(Two rooms: a sitting room stage right and a bedroom stage left with a connecting door that swings open into the bedroom. Up center in each room is a door to the corridor. In the sitting room, a large window [facing a street, several stories below], and a door to the kitchenette. In the bedroom, two more doors, both along the outside wall, one [upstage] to the closet, the other [downstage] to the bathroom. Six doors in all. The furniture consists, at a minimum, of a sofa, pouf, radio, and coffee table in the sitting room; and a bed and bureau in the bedroom.)

(As the house lights go down, we hear music: a recording of "O mio babbino caro," from Puccini's Gianni Schicchi, *sung thrillingly by a world-class soprano.)*

(When the lights come up, **JERRY**, *early thirties, is alone on stage. He's a good-looking fellow and adores opera. He sits listening rapturously to the opera – which by now is coming from the radio [and now sounds*

*scratchy as on an old recording]. He is
entirely caught up in the sensual sound of the
soprano's voice. He sways to the music and
mouths the words.)*

(After several seconds, **JO***, late twenties,
enters the sitting room from the corridor.
She's the assistant to the General Manager of
the Cleveland Grand Opera Company. She
makes an effort, but as always, she's a bit
scruffy, hair askew, without much makeup,
and she wears glasses. She enters hurriedly,
with urgency.)*

JO. Jerry!

JERRY. Shhh!

JO. Did she call?!

JERRY. No. Would you wait!

> *(***JO*** sighs. She looks at her watch. Then she
> notices* **JERRY***'s reaction to the music; he's
> swaying in rapture. When the aria ends,*
> **JERRY** *groans with pleasure.)*

RADIO ANNOUNCER. *The magnificent voice of soprano
Elena Firenzi, brought to you in honor of her live
appearance this evening with the Cleveland Grand
Opera Company.*

> *(***JO*** turns off the radio.)*

JO. She wasn't on the train.

JERRY. Oh my God, she is so amazing. When she hits that
high A-flat, I almost can't breathe.

JO. Jerry, she wasn't there!

> *(Ring! The phone rings.* **JO** *grabs it.)*

Hello?

No, ma'am, I couldn't find her.

(*To* **JERRY**.) It's your mother.

(*Into the phone.*) I-I-I don't know, Mrs. Wylie. I looked everywhere. I asked the conductor and I had her paged, I-I-I'm sorry, I just –

> (*Click.*)

Ma'am? ...Mrs. Wylie?

> (**JO** *hangs up.*)

She's gonna kill me.

JERRY. Oh come on, Jo. It's not your fault!

JO. Jerry, our star is two hours late. The rehearsal starts in ten minutes.

JERRY. She'll be here, Jo. It's Elena Firenzi. She's a genius. They just don't think like other people.

JO. So what are you saying? She's a grown woman. She can't tell time?

JERRY. Hey, I'm just not worried, okay?

> (*Beat.*)

And my God, just think of it. Tonight, the curtain rises, the spotlight hits her, and there's nothing else in the world but that voice.

JO. ...I can sing too, you know.

JERRY. Aw, Jo.

JO. I *can*! I can do it. I take voice lessons. And projection. And fencing! I'm good at fencing –

JERRY. I know you are.

JO. And I could be great. It just takes time.

JERRY. But Elena's a star, Jo. She sings all over the world. She was on the cover of *Life* magazine!

JO. So was Joseph Stalin!

JERRY. Look, all I'm saying is she's a great artist and she wouldn't just not show up. She's very sensitive.

JO. How do you know?

JERRY. *(Caught.)* Because I met her. Last year.

JO. You did? You never told me that.

JERRY. It was no big deal. When I was in Italy, I went to La Scala and she was in *Tosca*. Then afterwards I went backstage and well, there she was, all by herself, behind the curtain. She was wearing this sort of...negligee, and her whole body was glistening with sweat.

> *(His mouth is dry.)*

Anyway, she looked up and saw me and do you know what she did, Jo? She took my hand, put it to her cheek and just...held it there.

JO. What for?

JERRY. It was a gesture of art. And humanity. A sort of universal show of fellowship.

JO. She wanted sex, you idiot.

JERRY. Oh stop it.

JO. She's known for it! She likes men in their twenties. All young and succulent. She's like a vampire.

JERRY. I thought she was married.

JO. She is, but you know the Italians. They try the spaghetti, they try the linguine. So what else happened?

JERRY. Nothing! ...Of any importance.

JO. Something sort of happened?

JERRY. Not really.

JO. Jerry –

JERRY. It wasn't important.

JO. What happened?!

JERRY. *(Reluctantly; embarrassed.)* Oh, I...fainted.

JO. You fainted?

JERRY. Yes! It must have been the heat and all the excitement. I remember thinking suddenly, it's like an oven back here, and she was holding my hand to her cheek, and I held *her* hand to *my* cheek, and it was all these hands and cheeks, and then I blacked out. I think I took her down with me.

JO. Oh, great. This is terrific. My fiancé meets this sweaty naked Italian woman and he keels over.

JERRY. From the heat! Wait...fiancé?

JO. Yes, Jerry. Don't you remember? What did you, black out during the proposal?

JERRY. What are you talking about?

JO. Our *big date*. At the lake at Christmas. All that bracing air. We talked about marriage.

JERRY. Yes, we *talked* about it, but I'm just not ready to settle down yet, Jo. I want something different. Something exotic and romantic.

JO. I'm not romantic? Are you kidding me? What do you call a rowboat at three a.m., huh? Nobody for miles.

JERRY. You lost the oars.

JO. But it was fun. It turned out fun.

JERRY. We spent ten hours in a rowboat, Jo. On Christmas. The Coast Guard came with thermal blankets with little reindeer on them.

JO. That's not the point!

JERRY. Oh come on, Jo. I'm a lawyer. Our idea of a party is wearing colorful ties. But I want more than that.

JO. Well so do I. I'm in opera! We have flings and stuff.

JERRY. Flings?

JO. Well that's what you want, isn't it? A fling, like Leo?

JERRY. Who's Leo?

JO. Our tenor. He's from Amsterdam. He's flinging his way through the whole cast. All the sopranos are getting flung out. They call him the Flying Dutchman.

JERRY. Listen, Jo, let's be honest. When we kiss each other, do you hear anything special?

JO. Like what?

JERRY. Like...fireworks.

JO. Fireworks?

JERRY. Yeah.

JO. You mean like Flaming Pinwheels or just little sparklers?

JERRY. Jo –

JO. Or Roman Candles with the big ba-boom at the end.

JERRY. Forget it.

JO. Jerry –

JERRY. I said forget it!

(*A knock at the door.*)

MRS. WYLIE. (*Offstage.*) Jo!

JO. Coming!

(**JO** *opens the door and* **LUCILLE WYLIE** *enters. She's a force of nature. She's in her* *mid-fifties, well dressed, with great hair. She's a businesswoman in the 1930s, which in those days took the confidence of a Mack truck. She's extravagant, outspoken, crazy as a loon, and she doesn't like taking no for an answer. Think Carol Channing or Emma Thompson.)*

MRS. WYLIE. Well? Any word?

JO. Not yet.

MRS. WYLIE. Goddammit to hell! It's a phone, for God's sake! She can't use a phone?! Is she Amish?

JO. I-I-I'm sorry.

JERRY. Jo!

MRS. WYLIE. *(To* **JERRY.***)* What are *you* doing here?

JERRY. I'm sure I can be here if I want to.

MRS. WYLIE. Wrong.

JERRY. Mother –

MRS. WYLIE. Do you know what time it is?

JO. It's almost one.

MRS. WYLIE. Do you know what that means?

JO. She's late.

MRS. WYLIE. *It means she's late!*

> **(MRS. WYLIE** *takes a grape from the fruit bowl.)*

JO. I-I wouldn't worry, ma'am. I mean, I'm sure she'll get here.

MRS. WYLIE. Do I seem worried, Jo?

JO. No! No.

JERRY. Jo!

JO. I mean, well, yeah. You do.

MRS. WYLIE. I do? How interesting. In that case perhaps you can tell us what extrasensory, Jo-ellian perception has led you to form this startling and erroneous conclusion.

(*She pops the grape in her mouth.*)

JO. That – that's wax fruit.

(**MRS. WYLIE** *blows the grape across the room.*)

MRS. WYLIE. *Goddammit!*

JO. I'm sorry!

MRS. WYLIE. Call the station!

JO. I was just there.

MRS. WYLIE. *Then call the station!*

JO. Yes, ma'am.

(*She goes to the phone, finds the phone book, and looks for the number.*)

JERRY. Mother, have you taken your pills yet today?

MRS. WYLIE. Yes.

JERRY. You're lying, mother.

(*He pulls a bottle of pills from his pocket.*)

MRS. WYLIE. Listen, you. I pushed you out of these loins for six hours. I could have flown to Europe faster. And I don't need phenobarbital!

JERRY. Open wide.

MRS. WYLIE. Gerald –

JERRY. Mouth!

(He puts a pill on her tongue, and just as she swallows it: Ring! The telephone. They all freeze, then **JO** *reaches for it.)*

MRS. WYLIE. No! She's been in an accident. I can feel it.

(Ring!)

She's lying drunk in the gutter with her pantyhose on her head.

(Ring!)

All right! Pick it up!

JO. Hello? ...Yes it is... Oh no. That's terrible.

MRS. WYLIE. She's dead. Selfish diva.

JO. It's Mrs. Leverett. The rehearsal's starting.

MRS. WYLIE. Give me that!

(She grabs the phone; suddenly charming.)

Madam Chairwoman, how very kind of you to c–... No, no, she hasn't quite arrived yet... Jul–...Jul–...Julia! Will you calm down! ...What? ...I see. Well, if I may, I will leave that decision in your capable hands.

(She hangs up.)

It appears that the Opera Guild Collation Committee has decided to serve shrimp mayonnaise at the intermission, the refrigerator has broken down and the temperature backstage is a hundred degrees.

JO. So what do we do?

MRS. WYLIE. We play it by ear. If the shrimp stays pink, the donors get it. If it turns green, we feed it to the stagehands.

JO. Shall I call the station?

MRS. WYLIE. No. I've changed my mind. I want the line open.

(*To* **JERRY**.) And I want you out of here.

JERRY. Why?

MRS. WYLIE. Because I'm your mother.

JERRY. Mother –

MRS. WYLIE. Go practice law and prey on the helpless.

JERRY. Hey!

MRS. WYLIE. Out.

JERRY. I'll wait in the bedroom.

MRS. WYLIE. Wrong.

JERRY. But it's Elena Firenzi!

MRS. WYLIE. So what?

JERRY. She's my idol!

MRS. WYLIE. *It's the biggest night of my life and my son is standing here drooling on the rug!*

JERRY. Jo thinks I should stay. Don't you, Jo?

JO. ...I-I think your mother is right.

JERRY. Thanks a lot.

JO. I'm sorry!

> (**JERRY** *spots the room key on the table. Without them seeing it, he takes it with him.*)

JERRY. (*Ignoring* **JO**.) See you later, *Mother.*

> (*He exits, closing the door behind him.* **JO** *is miserable.*)

MRS. WYLIE. Time.

JO. One-fifteen.

MRS. WYLIE. I've got a thousand of Cleveland's so-called cognoscenti arriving at the theatre in six hours in black tie, a thirty piece orchestra, twenty-four chorus, fifteen stagehands and eight principals. Backstage, I have approximately fifty pounds of rotting shrimp mayonnaise, which, if consumed, could turn the Gala Be-A-Sponsor Buffet into a mass murder. All I don't have is a soprano.

JO. I'm-I'm really sorry, ma'am. I wish there was something I could do to help.

MRS. WYLIE. It's not your fault, Jo. I wish it was. The question now is what to do if prima donna cadenza doesn't arrive in time.

JO. I...I have an idea about that, actually.

MRS. WYLIE. You do?

JO. Yeah. I mean, sort of.

MRS. WYLIE. Well spit it out, Jo. And it better be good.

JO. Well, the thing is, I mean, I was just-just thinking that well, I mean...I could do it.

MRS. WYLIE. Do what?

JO. Sing it. Carmen. Sort of step in. You see, I-I've been to all the rehearsals and I know the part, and I-I mean, I could do it. I know I could.

MRS. WYLIE. Carmen?

JO. Yes, ma'am.

MRS. WYLIE. Spanish woman. Huge knockers.

JO. Yeah.

MRS. WYLIE. Carmen, Jo. She's a force of nature. She sucks men up like they're chicken with salsa. She has a body like the Rio Grande. It just keeps flowing. She goes through lovers like they're chunks of raw meat, and when she's had enough, she laughs at Don José until he stabs her to death with a butcher knife and she cries out to the gods in defiance and anger "*Take me! Take me to hell! I'm ready for you!!*"

It isn't you, Jo.

JO. It-it could be. I mean, if I had the chance.

MRS. WYLIE. *(Turning directly front, addressing the audience.)* "Ladies and gentlemen. May I have your attention, please. I regret to inform you that Miss Elena Firenzi, the greatest soprano of her generation, scheduled to make her American debut with the Cleveland Grand Opera Company in honor of our tenth anniversary season, is regrettably indisposed this evening, but...BUT! ...I have the privilege to announce that the role of Carmen will be sung tonight by a somewhat gifted amateur making her very first appearance on this, or indeed, any other stage, our company's very own factotum, gofer and all-purpose dogsbody, Jo!" Do you see the problem?

JO. I guess so.

MRS. WYLIE. Old men would be trampled to death in the stampede up the aisles.

JO. I see what you mean.

MRS. WYLIE. Time.

JO. One-twenty.

> *(A depressed silence.)*

> *(**MRS. WYLIE** picks up a grape and starts chewing – then spits it out. Ring!)*

Hello? ...What? Could you speak more slowly, please?

MRS. WYLIE. If it's Julia, tell her she can take the shrimp and stuff it up her –

JO. Ma'am! It's her! Elena. She's in the lobby!

MRS. WYLIE. *Yes!*

> *(She grabs the phone.)*

Signora Firenzi! *Benvenuto a Cleveland!* Did you have a *buen viaje? Molto benissimo? Benedetto journalé?* ...Jesus Christ, what am I saying? ...I will be down the stairs *immediamente. Molto fastissimo. Quicko instanto.* Jo, would you stop me!

> *(She hangs up.)*

All right, Jo. This is it. You have your instructions. Key word, Jo.

JO. Glue.

MRS. WYLIE. Glue. You will stick to her like

JO. glue.

MRS. WYLIE. And you will not let her out of your

JO. sight.

MRS. WYLIE. You will drive her to rehearsal and then drive her back. You will give her whatever she wants except

JO. liquor and men.

MRS. WYLIE. At the performance, you will lead a spontaneous

JO. standing ovation

MRS. WYLIE. then return her to the reception, keeping her

JO. sober

MRS. WYLIE. with her hands

JO. to herself

MRS. WYLIE. at which point she can

JO. drop dead

MRS. WYLIE. for all we care. Good.

JO. Good.

> (**MRS. WYLIE** *hurries to the door to the corridor.*)

MRS. WYLIE. Jo!

JO. Ma'am?

MRS. WYLIE. Get rid of the fruit.

> (**MRS. WYLIE** *exits, pulling the door closed behind her. Simultaneously,* **JERRY** *enters quickly through the bedroom/corridor door and closes it quietly. Then he darts to the bathroom and enters it, slamming the door behind him in his haste.* **JO** *hears the noise and stops, puzzled. Still holding the fruit, she walks into the bedroom and looks around. No one there. She goes to the bathroom door, opens it, and* **JERRY**, *who was holding the doorknob inside, is yanked into the room.*)

JO. *(Horrified.)* Jerry!

JERRY. Is she here?

JO. No! But she's coming up!

JERRY. Terrific!

JO. Jerry, do you realize what this looks like? Waiting for her in the bathroom?

> (*A knock at the front door.*)

She's here!

JERRY. Jo!

JO. With your mother!

JERRY. Bye Jo.

(He steps back into the bathroom and closes the door.)

JO. Jerry!

MRS. WYLIE. *(Offstage.)* Jo. The door is locked, Jo.

JO. Coming!

(She heads for the sitting room, then stops, realizing that she still has the fruit.)

Jerry! Door!

*(**JERRY** comes out, annoyed.)*

JERRY. Jo!

JO. Fruit!

JERRY. What?

JO. *Fruit!*

(She hands it to him.)

JERRY. *(Touched, accepting it.)* Aw, thanks, Jo.

*(He steps back in and **JO** slams the door.)*

MRS. WYLIE. *(Offstage.)* Jo!

JO. Coming!

*(She rushes into the sitting room, closing the connecting door. At the front door she stops abruptly. Adjusts herself. Opens the door. **MRS. WYLIE** enters.)*

MRS. WYLIE. *(Offstage – then on.)* JO!

JO. Hi.

MRS. WYLIE. *(Glaring murderously, then smiling broadly.)* Thank you, my darling, how very kind.

(She steps aside, permitting **ELENA** *and* **PASQUALE FIRENZI** *to enter the sitting room.* **ELENA** *is a force of nature. Gorgeous, nay, magnificent, and dressed to the nines.* **PASQUALE** *is a worthy consort, handsome and impressive.* **PASQUALE** *wears an overcoat with a big fur collar that you can't forget. They look like a magazine cover. Both of them speak of course with Italian accents.)*

MRS. WYLIE. My friends, your suite.

ELENA. So are you, I'm a-sure.

(She flings her hat, coat, and fur stole at **JO**.*)*

MRS. WYLIE. Thank you. I'll make the introductions, shall I? The *Buenos Díases.* The *Holas Que Tals.* The *Como Estandes Hoy Dia in Roma.* Oh God...

(She holds her head.)

This is Elena's husband, Pasquale, whom we did not expect, but could not possibly be more pleased to have with us. And this is his wife, the incomparable Elena Firenzi, who needs no introduction, yet I seem to be making one anyway. My assistant, Jo.

PASQUALE. John.

ELENA. John.

JO. Uh, Jo.

MRS. WYLIE. *(Enunciating.)* Jo.

ELENA. John!

JO. *(Shrugging.)* She can call me John if she wants.

PASQUALE. My wife would like a-da John. She throw up.

*(**JERRY** sticks his head out of the bathroom to see what's happening.)*

MRS. WYLIE. Oh the *john*. Yes of course. Right this way.

ELENA. Grazie.

> (*ELENA and* **MRS. WYLIE** *head for the john.*)

JO. The john. We-we misunderstood, you see, we usually say the STOP!!

> (**JERRY** *freezes.* **MRS. WYLIE** *and* **ELENA** *stop. They haven't entered the bedroom yet, but* **ELENA** *has opened the connecting door part-way.*)

There-there's one in the lobby. It's much prettier. Cleaner.

MRS. WYLIE. Are you all right, Jo?

JO. Me? Fine. I just...they've got this lovely ladies' room in the lobby. It has doilies.

MRS. WYLIE. I'm sure that this one is swell, Jo.

JO. No. No it isn't. Trust me.

ELENA. John!

MRS. WYLIE. Right this way, my dear.

> (**JERRY** *rushes into the closet, closing the door behind him just as* **MRS. WYLIE** *and* **ELENA** *head into the bedroom.*)

PASQUALE. Forgive a-my wife. *She's a-stupid!*

ELENA. *SHUT UP!*

PASQUALE. *SHUT UP A-YOUSELF!*

> (*Bang!* **ELENA** *enters the bathroom and slams the door behind her.*)

(*Continuing, to* **JO.**) She eats a-like a child, eh? We have food on the train. American food, it's all a-greasy.

And she eats a-too much. A ham*boorger*, a hot dog. I tell her stop, it make a-you sick, she say mind a-you business. So the waiter come by, Mr. Hot a-Stuff with his tight a-pants and he give her the eyeball and he say "You wanna my French fry, heh-heh?" and she say "Sure, I *like* a-you French fry, heh-heh, and how's a-you tater-tot" *and now she throws up!*

(*There's a knock at the front door.*)

MRS. WYLIE. Excuse me.

(**MRS. WYLIE** *opens the door to find the* **BELLHOP**, *who enters carrying two suitcases and a vanity case.*)

(*She's dressed in a traditional bellhop outfit.*)

BELLHOP. Luggage for Miss Firenzi! *La la laaaaaa!*

MRS. WYLIE. Shut up!

BELLHOP. Where is she?! I need to meet her!

MRS. WYLIE. You are not meeting her. Luggage in the bedroom, thank you.

BELLHOP. Yes, ma'am!

(**JO** *leads her to the bedroom.*)

MRS. WYLIE. (*To* **PASQUALE**.) I'm awfully sorry about that. You'd think that people would have better manners.

PASQUALE. Hey, it's okay. Is no big deal. It happens a-ten times a day. Phone rings, I pick it up, I get *La Bohème*. I go to the barber, he cut a-my hair, he sing me *Aida*.

(*Ring!*)

BELLHOP. (*Singing at the bathroom door, through the keyhole, riffing on "Largo al factotum."*) *Laaa – lalalalalalalalala – la – laaa*

JO. Hey!

MRS. WYLIE. *(Into the phone.)* Yes? ...Hello, Julia. Yes, she is...

(**MRS. WYLIE** *turns her back and, during the following, carries on a silent conversation with Julia.)*

(As **JO** *lays the fur stole and Elena's hat and coat on the bed, the* **BELLHOP** *opens the closet door, revealing* **JERRY** *standing in the doorway. However, she doesn't see him, having turned away to get the suitcases.* **JO**, *however, sees* **JERRY** *and slams the door.)*

(The **BELLHOP** *looks up, sees that* **JO** *has slammed the door and sighs at* **JO** *with annoyance. She returns to the closet door and opens it again and turns away without seeing* **JERRY***. As she picks up the two suitcases,* **JERRY** *runs out of the closet and hides behind the closet door.)*

(As the **BELLHOP** *enters the closet with the suitcases,* **JO** *opens the bedroom/corridor door and motions to* **JERRY** *to leave. He sticks his head out from behind the closet door and shakes it "no." As the* **BELLHOP** *reenters from the closet, he disappears again.)*

(The **BELLHOP** *goes to the bed and gathers up the stole, coat, and hat – at which point,* **JERRY** *runs around the closet door and back into the closet, slamming the door behind him. This is followed immediately by* **JO** *slamming the corridor door. The* **BELLHOP** *looks at one door, then the other, then at* **JO**, *who feigns innocence, as though nothing has happened.)*

*(The **BELLHOP** shrugs and opens the closet door and **JERRY** is standing there. She stares at him for a moment; then wordlessly, she hands him the hat, coat, and fur. He nods as if to say "thank you" and the closes the door. Then the **BELLHOP** gives **JO** a "thumbs up" and hits her on the arm as if to say "way to go." Then she goes into the sitting room followed by **JO**, who closes the connecting door behind her.)*

MRS. WYLIE. *(Continued; into the phone.)* Julia, as soon as possible! ...No, she's fine... Julia, she is perfectly all right!

*(**BELLHOP** comes over with her hand out. **MRS. WYLIE** hands her a coin.)*

BELLHOP. *(Looking at the tip.)* She's got to be kidding.

MRS. WYLIE. Out! Now! Goodbye, Julia.

(She hangs up.)

BELLHOP. My sister's a bellhop in Tomball and she gets bigger tips than this.

MRS. WYLIE. I believe you owe this man an apology.

BELLHOP. I do?

MRS. WYLIE. I would say so, yes.

BELLHOP. Fine.

*(To **PASQUALE**.)* Signor, mi dispiace. Non volevo disturbarla. Se l'ho offesa, chiedo scusa, chiedo scusa. *(Nodding at **MRS. WILEY**.)* Questa donna è *stupida*, ch'è *un idiota*, è *molto economica*.

[Sir, I'm sorry. I did not intend to bother you. If I have offended you, I certainly beg your forgiveness. This woman is *stupid, an idiot* and *very cheap*.]

PASQUALE. Non e niente, l'assicuro.

[I assure you, it's of no importance.]

BELLHOP. Grazie lo salute.

PASQUALE. Ciao.

BELLHOP. Ciao.

>*(The **BELLHOP** gives **MRS. WYLIE** a look, then exits to the corridor, closing the door behind her.)*

JO. I hope Signora Firenzi is all right.

PASQUALE. Phh!

>*(At this point **ELENA** emerges from the bathroom, holding the fruit bowl, puzzled by it. She looks sick. She puts it on the bureau, then sits on the bed.)*

MRS. WYLIE. I don't suppose this sort of thing affects her singing. I mean she will go on?

PASQUALE. You got a-men in the opera?

MRS. WYLIE. Men? Well yes, of course. Fourteen.

PASQUALE. She wouldn't miss it, believe me. You know why? Eh? She likes a-men 'cause they got a-that *thing*. *(Gropes.)* A-what's a-the word. Starts a-with P.

MRS. WYLIE. P?

JO. Pride?

MRS. WYLIE. Personality?

PASQUALE. All men, they got this thing. It starts a-small, it gets a-big, and it makes a-trouble.

MRS. WYLIE. P?

JO. Persistence?

PASQUALE. Passion! She's likes a-big a-passion!

JO. Oh.

MRS. WYLIE. I see.

(**ELENA** *enters the sitting room.*)

JO. Signora Firenzi!

MRS. WYLIE. Are you all right?

ELENA. Me? I'm a-fine. Perfetta...

PASQUALE. Hoo.

ELENA. I'm a-tip-a-top. I feel like ten bucks.

PASQUALE. Liar!

ELENA. Shut up! A little stomach. Is nothing. I'm a-fine. A few more minutes, I'm gonna be even better.

MRS. WYLIE. Better?

PASQUALE. That's what I thought. I get a-you pills.

(*He heads for the bedroom to get her pills. The following argument just keeps escalating.*)

ELENA. I done take pills.

PASQUALE. You need a-pills!

ELENA. No! I'm a-Firenzi! Firenzi says a-no!

PASQUALE. What's a-matter? You got a man in there?

ELENA. Yeah. Sure. I got a man. In fact, I got two men. Both a-naked. Go ahead, look!

PASQUALE. Phhh!

ELENA. Pazzo!

PASQUALE. Strega!

ELENA. Idiota!

PASQUALE. *Puttana!*

ELENA. Someday, you gonna wake up in a-you bed, you gonna be the *soprano!*

> *(They both start yelling.* **ELENA** *is appealing to* **JO**, **PASQUALE** *is appealing to* **MRS. WYLIE**. *All overlapping:)*

Jealousy, eh? He's a-jealous of me! It's a-terrible!

PASQUALE. *In my heart, she makes a-me crazy.*

ELENA. *He's a crazy man.*

PASQUALE. *She don't think about what I'm a-doin'!*

ELENA. *His whole life is a-crazy a-jealousy, jealousy –*

PASQUALE. *SHUT UP!*

ELENA. *SHUT UP A-YOUSELF!*

> *(Bang!* **PASQUALE** *slams into the bedroom and sits on the bed.* **ELENA** *fumes.)*

MRS. WYLIE. Well that was cleansing. So, I don't mean to be pushy, but I really do think we ought to be going.

ELENA. Sure. Thanks a-for everything. See you tonight.

MRS. WYLIE. No. Sorry. I meant all of us. To the rehearsal.

ELENA. Me?

MRS. WYLIE. Right.

ELENA. No, I done think so. You want the truth, I'm not so good.

MRS. WYLIE. You're not?

ELENA. No.

MRS. WYLIE. What's the matter?

ELENA. I'm a-sick. I eat a ham*boorger*. I'm a-stupid.

MRS. WYLIE. Signora Firenzi. I don't think you understand. I have a hundred people at the theatre. Cento persona numeroso. They're waiting for you.

ELENA. Hey. You done get it. I'm gonna sing right now. I'm gonna throw up on the tenor.

MRS. WYLIE. *But I could sue you.*

ELENA. *If I'm in a-da ground, good luck collecting!* Hey! Done worry, okay? Tonight I'm gonna be there. I'm a-Firenzi. I done miss performance.

MRS. WYLIE. But you don't know the stage directions! The tempos!

ELENA. I sing *Carmen* a hundred times. Is no big deal.

MRS. WYLIE. And what about the costume fitting?!

ELENA. I bring a-my own. It's in the suitcase. You wanna see? In fact, I bring a-two costumes. Just in case.

MRS. WYLIE. You can't do this.

ELENA. I wear my own costume at Vienna Staatsoper, Covent Garden. You think in Cleveland I'm gonna suffer?

(*Ring!* **MRS. WYLIE** *grabs it.*)

MRS. WYLIE. Yes? ...*Oh my God!* I'll be right there. Just keep looking! ...Jul...Juli...*Julia, don't panic!*

(*She hangs up.*)

JO. Trouble?

MRS. WYLIE. They lost the music. All of it.

ELENA. That's not good.

MRS. WYLIE. All right, now listen. I want an answer and I want it now. Are you coming or not?

ELENA. Not.

MRS. WYLIE. Right. That's settled. Jo!

JO. Ma'am?

MRS. WYLIE. If there's a problem of any kind, I want you to call me immediately.

JO. Yes, ma'am.

MRS. WYLIE. I'll be at the theatre.

JO. Right.

(**ELENA** *groans.*)

MRS. WYLIE. Jo!

(*She motions for* **JO** *to join her at the door.*)

JO. Ma'am?

MRS. WYLIE. She needs some sleep. Do whatever you have to. Hit her with a chair when she isn't looking.

JO. Yes, ma'am.

(**MRS. WYLIE** *exits.* **ELENA** *leans back on the sofa. She doesn't notice at first that* **JO** *is still there; then she does.*)

ELENA. You stay here?

JO. Yes. I-I-I mean if you don't mind.

ELENA. Sure. Help a-youself.

(*She belches.*)

Scusi. That's a-the tater tot.

JO. You really are sick, aren't you?

ELENA. Is okay. I'm gonna live. In my village, they gotta saying. "Nobody ever dies from a-gas." And believe me, they know.

JO. But maybe you should take those pills. I mean, they might help.

ELENA. Thanks, a-no. I need sleep, not a-pills. I gotta relax. Take a deep breath. Is not so easy, eh?

JO. Why not?

ELENA. Why not. Today it's a-Cleveland. Monday New York. Rushing every place. I live in hotels. If I ever have babies they'll be delivered by room service.

JO. I'm sorry.

ELENA. When I'm a-tense, I feel a-sick, then I can't sing nothing.

JO. Nothing?

ELENA. Singing is like a-life, eh? You gotta relax, take it easy. You get a-tense, you finished.

JO. I know what you mean. I-I sing myself, a little.

ELENA. You?

JO. Yeah. I-I-I mean, not like you. I wish I could.

ELENA. Hey. Done knock youself down. Is no good. To sing, you need a-confidence. You gotta say I'm a-the best. I'm a-Jo. I sing good.

JO. I'm the best. I'm Jo. I sing good. But the trouble is, whenever I sing in front of people, I get tense. I-I tighten up. I can't help it.

ELENA. That's it, eh? That's a-me, now. My doctor, he say take a-pills. Phenobarbital. It makes-a you sleep. But I'm-a Firenzi. I done take a-pills!

JO. *(To herself.)* Phenobarbital.

> *(During the following, **JO** picks up Mrs. Wylie's bottle of phenobarbital from the table, where Jerry left it.)*

ELENA. Hey! I got it. We have a drink. You want a martini?

JO. Hm? No! No, I-I-I don't think that's such a –

(She looks at the bottle of pills.)

Well. All right.

ELENA. You got a-glasses?

JO. I-I-I don't know.

ELENA. You're gonna join me.

(She heads for the bedroom.)

JO. Right. Okay. One drink.

*(**JO** disappears into the kitchenette as **ELENA** enters the bedroom. **PASQUALE** is lying on the bed, on his stomach, reading a car magazine.)*

ELENA. Ciao.

PASQUALE. Ciao.

(He ignores her. Sniffs.)

ELENA. Hey. Mia vongole. I'm a-sorry, okay?

PASQUALE. Phh. It done matter. You're the star, eh?

ELENA. Pasquale. Done be like that. You're a-*my* star, okay?

PASQUALE. Phh.

ELENA. Hey, listen. We take a vacation, soon.

(She sits on the bed.)

Greece, eh? We get a boat. We sail a-the islands. Sleep all day on the sand.

(She's rubbing his back, then his backside.)

PASQUALE. Oh, *belleza*.

ELENA. Just a-two, eh. Like a-the old days.

PASQUALE. Clams.

ELENA. Oysters!

PASQUALE. Big a-lobster.

ELENA. Ooo.

PASQUALE. We suck a-da claws,

ELENA. And pull a-da tail.

PASQUALE. Now close a-da door.

ELENA. Huh?

PASQUALE. Close a-door.

ELENA. Now?

PASQUALE. Close.

ELENA. Pasquale. I got a stomach. No joke.

PASQUALE. I make a-you better. Fix you up.

ELENA. No. Hey. Not now. Okay? Hey-hey, I can't do it!

    (He stops, angry.)

PASQUALE. You got a man.

ELENA. I got nobody.

PASQUALE. You got a man, so done lie!

ELENA. Pasquale –

PASQUALE. There has been nothing for two days! Not once, eh?

ELENA. I'm sorry. I get a-tense. I got a stomach.

PASQUALE. I wanna be a monk, I'll join a-the church! At least, sometimes, I have a-some fun. I pluck a-da chickens. Sing a-da hymns.

ELENA. He's crazy. My husband's a-crazy.

PASQUALE. Oh sure, I'm a-crazy. I hate a-trains, I'm a-crazy. I hate hotels. I'm a-crazy. I got a-empty bed and I'm a-crazy!

ELENA. Pasquale, I'm a sick a-woman!

PASQUALE. SO TAKE A-YOU PILLS! YOUR PHENOBARBITAL!

ELENA. *(Angry.)* Fine. Okay. I take a-pills!

> *(She goes to the vanity case and takes out pills.)*

You wanna pills, I take a-pills. Look! Hey! Two pills. No. Four pills!

PASQUALE. Two!

ELENA. *Four!!*

PASQUALE. Pah!

ELENA. Okay? Happy?!

> *(She puts the bottle on the bedside table.)*

PASQUALE. Phh!

ELENA. I take a-pills, I got a happy husband. A happy marriage!

> *(She pulls a bottle of vodka and a cocktail shaker from the vanity case.)*

PASQUALE. Now you gonna be sick.

ELENA. So what? My fella in the closet, he's not gonna care.

PASQUALE. Pazza!

ELENA. SHUT UP!

PASQUALE. SHUT UP A-YOUSELF!

(Bang! Bang! **PASQUALE** *slams into the bathroom.* **ELENA** *slams into the sitting room.)*

ELENA. Jo!

(She paces, upset. **JO** *enters from the kitchenette with two martini glasses.)*

JO. Are you all right?

ELENA. I'm a-peachy. I'm a-fine. I done relax, I'm a-gonna blow up! Here!

(She hands **JO** *the bottle and shaker.)*

JO. *(Taking it and reading the label.)* Vodka?

ELENA. Phh! I forget the Vermouth. Done move.

*(***ELENA** *enters the bedroom, grabs the suitcase, and looks for the vermouth. As she does,* **JO** *unscrews the top from the bottle of phenobarbital and pours several pills into one side of the cocktail shaker. She thinks for a moment, then pours more pills.)*

(By this time, **ELENA** *has found the vermouth. She slams back into the sitting room as* **JO** *pockets the bottle of pills. During the following,* **ELENA** *makes martinis in the shaker. She uses ice from the ice bucket.)*

Jealousy, eh? That's all I get is a-jealousy. Back a-stage, men come to a-see me. Good men. Fine men. They say "Elena, you are a great artist and you make us a-happy." That's all! That's it! And Pasquale, he goes a-crazy!

(By this time, **ELENA** *is shaking the shaker like it's Pasquale's throat, as hard as she can.)*

JO. I'll pour.

(**JO** *takes the shaker, fills* **ELENA**'s *glass and hands it to her. Then she puts her finger into* **ELENA**'s *glass and stirs in order to dissolve all the pills.* **ELENA** *watches, startled, then bemused. She looks at* **JO**. **JO** *removes her finger and acts as if nothing's wrong.*)

ELENA. Hey. You join me.

JO. Gee, I-I-I don't really –

ELENA. Drink!

JO. Right.

(**JO** *pours some martini into her own glass and raises it.*)

Well – down the hatch.

(*Ceremoniously, proud to know the local ritual,* **ELENA** *puts her finger into* **JO**'s *glass and stirs.*)

ELENA. Salut.

(**ELENA** *drains her glass as* **JO** *watches. For a moment,* **ELENA** *senses something strange; then she sighs with pleasure at the effect of the drink.* **JO** *is relieved.*)

JO. I think you're going to feel a lot better now.

ELENA. I hope so, eh? 'Cause worse would be impossible.

(**ELENA** *sits down heavily.*)

JO. You-you might even take a nap. Who knows...

ELENA. Sure. Who knows.

(*She picks up the shaker and starts pouring herself a second glass.*)

ELENA. Miracles happen, eh?

JO. *(Trying to stop her.)* Signora Firenzi, I-I-I –

ELENA. Elena! You call me Elena. 'Cause I like you.

JO. Uh, right. Elena.

> *(It's too late. The martini is poured.* **JO** *takes the shaker.)*

Nice and cold...

> *(She puts the shaker down as far from* **ELENA** *as possible.)*

ELENA. Salut.

> *(As* **ELENA** *drinks, the bathroom door swings open and* **PASQUALE** *stalks into the bedroom.)*

PASQUALE. *(To himself.)* No more! That's it! I'm a-finished with that woman!

> *(During the following, he finds a pen and a piece of paper, then sits on the bed and starts to write a farewell note to Elena. Meanwhile, in the sitting room:)*

ELENA. *(Relaxing.)* Hey. Jo. Sing a-me something.

JO. Huh?

ELENA. You sing, I listen. Maybe I help, eh? Make a-pointer.

JO. Gee, that's awfully... Now?

ELENA. Sure. Why not? Free lesson.

JO. Well, I-I-I suppose...

ELENA. Come on. Let's hear. Stand up!

JO. *(Standing.)* Right. Is there, uh, anything special?

ELENA. Pick a-you favorite. Go.

JO. Right.

> *(She's nervous and embarrassed. She clears
> her throat, then gropes for the right pitch.)*

Ahem. Okay.

> *(Without much confidence, she starts to sing.
> She's chosen the mezzo soprano line [Laura]
> for the duet "L'amo come il fulgor del creato,"
> from Act II, Scene Seven of Ponchielli's* La
> Gioconda. *She sings without accompaniment
> and not very well.)*

L'AMO COME IL FULGOR DEL CREATO!
COME L'AURA CHE AVVIVA IL RESPIRO!
COME IL SOGNO CELESTE E BEATO
DA CUI VENNE IL MIO PRIMO SOSPIR.

ELENA. Stop!

> *(**JO** stops.)*

Okay. You're a-tight, eh? Tense. Is no good. You gotta
relax. Be you.

JO. I-I-I'm trying. I –

ELENA. Okay. Now expand a-you chest.

JO. My chest?

ELENA. Sure!

JO. Don't expect much.

ELENA. Like a-this.

> *(Standing erect, she does an exercise that
> expands her chest. It's a very good chest.)*

Mwhaaa! Mwhaaa!

JO. Right. Wa.

ELENA. No. *Mwhaaa! Mwhaaa!*

JO. *Mwhaa!*

ELENA. *Good!* Now shake-a-youself.

> *(She shakes her body, arms flailing – singer's exercise.)*

Come on! Relax.

> *(Tentatively,* **JO** *imitates her.)*

Move!

> *(***JO*** *lets loose. They both move around the room, arms flailing.)*

Good. Okay. Now the throat. It's a-tight. It's gotta be loose. Like this.

> *(She rolls her head in a circle around her shoulders, simultaneously singing a note.)*

Ahhh...

JO. Ahhh...

> *(***JO*** *does it but it makes her dizzy and she almost falls over.)*

ELENA. Good. Now all together.

> *(They sing "ah," roll their heads, and move around the room, arms flailing. After a few seconds,* **ELENA** *stops and watches* **JO***, who eventually notices that she's doing it alone. She straightens up.)*

(Continued.) Now – A trick, eh? You gotta hear the music. Before you sing. You gotta hear everything. The orchestra, the chorus –

JO. *(Enthusiastic.)* I-I know what you mean!

ELENA. And *then,* when you sing, with every word, you are surprised by life, and you say to yourself, "These feelings are new. I've not had them before. I am in awe of life, and now, as I sing, it is unfolding in front of me. It is a voyage of discovery and it gives me hope." And then you transform that hope, and love, and majesty by finding it all inside you. It is there, now show us. Shh. Listen.

> *(Silence. Then we hear four notes, pizzicato, from the orchestra – which is now in their heads. A fifth note swells and they begin the duet. We hear the orchestra in their heads. They sing a duet from* La Gioconda *and it becomes more and more confident and glorious.)*

> *(Singing Laura's part.)*

LAMO COME IL FULGOR DEL CREATO!
COME L'AURA CHE AVVIVA IL RESPIRO!
COME IL SOGNO CELESTE E BEATO
DA CUI VENNE IL MIO PRIMO SOSPIR.

JO. *(Singing Gioconda's part.)*

ED IO LAMO SICCOME IL LEONE
AMA IL SANGUE, ED IL TURBINE IL VOLO
E LA FOLGOR LE VETTE, E L'ALCIONE
LE VORAGINI, E L'AQUILA IL SOL!

ELENA & JO.

PEL SUO BACIO SOAVE IO DISFIDO
DELLA MORTE L'ORROR! *(Etc.)*

> *(Their duet gets progressively more confident and dramatic. Meanwhile, during the singing,* **PASQUALE,** *in the bedroom, stands, having finished his note. He scans it with tears in his eyes, folds it in half, and props it on the bed, on top of the pillow. Note: The paper*

*should be distinctive and easy to recognize –
lavender, perhaps. He picks up his suitcase,
heads for the door to the corridor, and opens
it. Then he stops. He forgot something – his
overcoat.)*

(He goes to the closet, opens it, and **JERRY**
*falls out, having fallen asleep inside, against
the door.* **JERRY** *is aghast.* **PASQUALE** *grabs
his coat with the big fur collar and exits, as*
JERRY *follows him off, trying to explain. This
is all in mime, during the duet –)*

*(Which then comes to a huge and wonderful
ending, filling the theater with sheer beauty:)*

ELENA & JO. *(Singing.)*
   PEL SUO BACIO SOAVE IO DISFIDO
   DELLA MORTE L'ORROR!

ELENA. Haha!

JO. Haha!

ELENA. That's a-so nice! That's a-gorgeous! You sing
a-gorgeous!

JO. *(Overlapping.)* I-I-I see what you mean! I felt so good!
I mean, I-I felt relaxed!

ELENA. Ohh! That was fun, eh? Whew!

JO. It was wonderful!

     (They calm down.)

ELENA. Hey. Guess what. I think I'm a-tired.

JO. Oh. I-I'm sorry. I –

ELENA. No! That's a-good. I'm gonna sleep.

JO. Oh. Oh good! That-that's great.

ELENA. *(Yawning.)* Yahh! Hoo.

(She stands up unsteadily.)

Jo. You wake a-me, eh? Six-thirty.

JO. Right. Sure. I promise.

*(**ELENA** heads for the bedroom.)*

Uh...Elena. Thanks for the lesson.

ELENA. Hey. You sing a-beautiful. No joke. You got real promise.

JO. Thanks.

ELENA. We talk a-more, later, okay?

JO. Sure. And if you need anything, just holler.

> *(**ELENA** goes into the bedroom and closes the door. **JO**, who feels wonderful, sits and daydreams.)*

> *(**ELENA** is exhausted now – drugged, in fact. She realizes that Pasquale isn't there. She looks around. She calls toward the bathroom.)*

ELENA. Pasquale! Hey. I'm gonna sleep. Okay?

> *(No answer. She shrugs, and with a groan, stretches out on the bed until she comes nose to nose with Pasquale's note. She picks it up and reads it. Beat. A scream.)*

EEEEEEEEEEEEEEE! NO! NO! NO!

> *(**ELENA** drops the note on the bedside table as **JO** bounds out of her chair and runs to the bedroom.)*

JO. What happened?!

ELENA. Impossible!

JO. What?!

ELENA. No!!

JO. WHAT HAPPENED?!

ELENA. He's a-gone! Pasquale!

JO. Gone where?

ELENA. *(Shaking* **JO.***)* Gone! Gone! He's a-gone!

JO. Elena!

ELENA. *(Releasing her.)* He's a-left me for good!

JO. Are you sure?

ELENA. HE'S A-GONE!

JO. Now-now-now wait a second. Maybe he went downstairs. For-for a magazine.

ELENA. Look! Look! No suitcase!

> *(She flings open the closet door.)*

No coat!

JO. I guess he's gone.

ELENA. PASQUALE!! NO! NO! NO!

JO. ELENA! CALM DOWN!

ELENA. *(Sitting, crying.)* Jo... Jo –

JO. Now listen! We-we-we can look for him. We'll look in the lobby –

ELENA. It's a-my fault. I'm a-never there. He's not a-happy. Me. I make him unhappy.

JO. Elena –

ELENA. He hates a-me. I wanna kill myself.

JO. He'll come back. You'll see.

ELENA. *I'm gonna kill myself!*

(She jumps up and runs into the sitting room.)

JO. Stop!

(JO runs after her. ELENA looks wildly around the room for her instrument of destruction. She picks up the shaker – no use. She tosses it away and JO catches it, still chasing her.)

ELENA. I'm gonna kill myself! I live a-no more!

JO. Calm down!

ELENA. No more!

JO. Hey, please!

ELENA. He hates a-me! I hate a-myself!

(ELENA rushes into the kitchenette.)

JO. No, Elena!

(JO follows her; noise of a struggle.)

(Offstage.) Elena, stop it!

ELENA. *(Offstage.)* Get away!

JO. *(Offstage.)* Don't! Hey!

(A crash – a drawer of cutlery hitting the floor. A second later ELENA runs out, followed by JO. ELENA is holding a fork.)

Elena!

ELENA. *I'm gonna kill myself!*

JO. *Put down that fork!*

ELENA. He hates a-me! It's all over!

JO. Elena! This is not an opera! Please! Put it down!

(ELENA drops the fork and collapses onto the sofa, exhausted.)

ELENA. Oh, Jo! *Jo!*

JO. It's all right. You'll be fine.

ELENA. He's a-gone.

JO. It's not your fault.

ELENA. Oh, Pasquale. Pasquale...

JO. He'll come back. You'll see.

> (**ELENA** *picks up the shaker and starts to drink.*)

Hey! Hey, no! Stop!

> (**JO** *takes the shaker.*)

Come on. Get up. Let's get you to bed.

ELENA. I can't.

JO. Let's go!

> (**JO** *pulls* **ELENA** *to her feet and, holding her up, leads her to the bedroom.*)

ELENA. Jo, he hates a-me.

JO. Nooo. He loves you. He'll come back.

ELENA. I wanna kill myself.

JO. Into bed. Come on.

> (*She lays* **ELENA** *down on the bed. Throughout the following,* **ELENA** *becomes increasingly limp and dizzy. Her speech slurs with exhaustion.*)

ELENA. Bed...

JO. You'll get a good sleep, you'll feel a lot better, I promise.

ELENA. Sleep...

JO. We'll take off your shoes...

(*She pulls* **ELENA***'s shoes off.*)

ELENA. Shoes...

JO. There. I'll bet that feels good, huh? Now close your eyes. I'll be right inside.

ELENA. Jo!

JO. What?!

ELENA. Jo, done leave me! Stay! Please!

JO. I will. I'm right here.

ELENA. Sleep...

JO. Shhh. That's right. A good sleep... off you go...

(*Pause. All is quiet.* **JO** *sits onto the edge of the bed.*)

ELENA. Jo!

JO. (*Falling off the bed.*) I'm right here!

ELENA. Jo... Sing me...

JO. Right.

(*She clears her throat.*)

Is there, uh, anything special –?

ELENA. Sing!

JO. Sing.

(**JO** *tries feebly to get the pitch, as before. Then she remembers the lesson and shuts her eyes to conjure up the orchestra. Four pizzicato notes sound the pitch in* **JO***'s head. She looks up and smiles. Then softly she begins to sing the aria "O del mio dolce ardor" from Gluck's* Paride ed Elena.)

JO. *(Singing.)*

O DEL MIO DOLCE ARDOR
BRAMATO OGGETTO
L'AURA CHE TU RESPIRE,
ALFIN RESPIRO

... *(Etc.)*

> *(As* **ELENA** *falls asleep she reaches for* **JO***'s hand and holds it.* **JO** *is taken aback for a second, then pats* **ELENA***'s hand and continues singing. The lights fade as the sound of the orchestra takes over the musical theme.)*

End of Scene

Scene Two

(Three hours later. About six-thirty p.m. JO and ELENA are asleep in different rooms. JO is in the sitting room on the sofa. ELENA is stretched out on the bed, under the covers. As the music fades, Ring! JO wakes up, disoriented. She answers the phone.)

JO. Hello?

BELLHOP. *(Through the phone, singing.) Laaa – lalalala lalalalala – la – laaa*

JO. Thank you –

BELLHOP. This is your bellhop. It's six-thirty! This is your wakeup call!

JO. Thanks.

BELLHOP. Now listen. I want to meet her.

JO. What?

BELLHOP. Elena Firenzi. La Stupenda! I can come upstairs.

JO. No. She's sleeping.

BELLHOP. But she's my idol. I have all her recordings. Don't you get it! I've admired her since I was a little bellhop. I need to meet her.

JO. I'm sorry.

BELLHOP. Please.

JO. No!

BELLHOP. Oh, please!

JO. *Not now!* ...

(The BELLHOP chokes back a sob. JO sighs.)

JO. Look. All right. If you bring up some coffee, you can meet her for a second.

BELLHOP. Yipppeeeeee!

(*Click. There's a knock at the front door.*)

JO. Coming!

(**JO** *goes to the door and opens it. It's* **LEO**. **LEO** *is the company's principal tenor. He's Dutch, from Amsterdam, and has a heavy Dutch accent. He's about twenty-eight, extremely handsome, sexy and self-confident with a beautiful smile and great warmth. His body is gorgeous, even with his clothes on. One can only imagine what it's like with his clothes off. Imagine a young Chris Hemsworth, or Brad Pitt in his early days.*)

Leo.

LEO. Hello, Jo.

(*He strolls in. Looks around.*)

Oooh, dis iss nice place, dis room. I could get used to all dis.

JO. Yeah. Well, you know. Elena Firenzi.

LEO. Of course I know. She is big-big opera star. Und I t'ink she vill adore me silly.

(**LEO** *wanders around the room, in no hurry.*)

JO. How was rehearsal?

LEO. Not zo good. Imagine me, the Flying Dutchman, playing Don José in *Carmen*. Und there was no Elena! Und believe me, it was not zo romantic singing der duets mitt der stagehand.

JO. Yeah, I'm-I'm sorry about that. She'll be there tonight, though. I promise.

LEO. And it vill vork zo much better dat vay.

　　　(He snorts.)

JO. Uh, Leo is there anything I can do for you?

LEO. Not really. I am stopping by to give Miss Firenzi a good Dutch Velcome, instead of meeting her on der stage tonight for der very first time.

JO. Gee, that's-that's nice of you, but the thing is, she's uh, she's sleeping right now. She's taking a nap.

LEO. *(Sitting.)* And I am fine mitt der vaiting and I am not in da hurry.

JO. Yeah, well – actually, I-I thought it might be better if I got her to the theatre first and then she could meet everybody, at the same time. I mean, I've got to wake her, and she has to get ready, and she might want some time alone. If you see what I mean.

LEO. Do you know vhat she could do for me, Jo?

JO. Well –

LEO. Yoost a single call from Miss Firenzi to New York Zity und bing bang boom, I vould be at der Metropolitan Opera in less than two – t'ree days.

JO. Well yeah, that's –

LEO. Four days tops.

JO. And that would –

LEO. Five days max if there's traffic on the Triborough Bridge.

JO. Right, I do see what you're –

LEO. So therefore, Jo, it is zo important to me dat she gets to know me both as zinger and as human being. I am voice und body. Are you seeing dis, Jo?

JO. Yeah, I am. I really am. Except right now, the thing is just to get her there, and-and then later, you'll have plenty of time with her, one-on-one, right? I mean she'll be here tomorrow. Right? Okay?

(*Beat; he puts the moves on her:*)

LEO. You are very good-looking voman, Jo. Has anyone told you dat before?

JO. Sure. My-my mother. My Aunt Harriet.

LEO. Anyone zingle?

JO. My cousin Ralphie. He's technically single. He's five.

LEO. You are not going to let me see her now, are you, Jo?

JO. Later. I promise. I'll-I'll arrange it so you have lots of time with her. Alone. I promise.

LEO. Vill you give her a message for me?

JO. Sure. Anything.

LEO. Tell her zis.

(*He kisses her on the lips. It's a very long kiss. She doesn't know what to do with her arms. She breaks it off.*)

JO. YAHH!! I'll tell her. Of course she might misunderstand.

LEO. Zee you later, Jo.

(*He exits, closing the door behind him.*)

JO. (*She looks at her watch.*) Oh jeez.

(*She hurries to the connecting door and knocks.*)

Elena. It's time to get up. Sorry.

> *(She opens the door and switches on the bedroom light, then heads back into the sitting room. During the following, she picks up the shaker and glasses and heads for the kitchenette as* **ELENA** *continues sleeping.)*

I ordered some coffee, but if you want anything else, I can call downstairs.

> *(***JO*** *goes into the kitchenette, then comes out again a moment later, having disposed of the bottle and glasses.)*

Are you hungry? Elena?

> *(No answer;* **JO** *goes to the connecting door, looks in the bedroom and sees that* **ELENA** *is still asleep.)*

Elena. It's time to get up. You'll be late.

> *(***JO*** *enters the bedroom and walks to the bed. She shakes* **ELENA**.*)*

Hey, come on. I hate to wake you, but it's quarter to seven.

> *(No response.)*

Elena, let's go!

> *(She pulls* **ELENA** *up by the arms and releases her.* **ELENA** *flops back on the bed.)*

What's the matter? Elena, wake up!

> *(She shakes her harder.)*

Elena!

(No response. **JO** *straightens up and stares at* **ELENA**, *suddenly afraid. She then notices a folded note on the bedside table – Pasquale's note, which happens to be next to Elena's bottle of pills. She picks up the note and reads it.)*

JO. "By the time you get this, I'll be gone forever."

*(***JO** *stiffens – looks at* **ELENA**, *then back at the note.)*

"After what has happened, it is just not worth to me the pain and unhappiness of staying around any more. The fun is gone, and now so am I."

(She stares at the note, horrified. She then sees the bottle of pills and picks it up. It's empty.)

Elena! Wake up!

(She shakes her violently.)

Elena, for God's sake!

(A knock at the front door. **JO** *doesn't hear it.)*

Elena, wake up! Please wake up! Please!

(Suddenly, **JO** *stops shaking her. She realizes that it's no use.* **ELENA** *is gone.* **JO** *is white as a sheet.)*

Oh my God.

MRS. WYLIE. *(Offstage; knocking.)* Open the door, Jo!

JO. *(Calling.)* C-coming! One second!

*(***JO** *looks at* **ELENA** *sadly. She's lost a friend.)*

Elena. I'm so sorry.

MRS. WYLIE. *(Offstage; knocking.)* Jo! Open the door!

*(**JO** turns away and walks into the sitting room, closing the connecting door behind her. She's in a daze, but makes it to the corridor door and opens it.)*

*(**MRS. WYLIE** enters in a gorgeous, expensive evening gown for the night's festivities.)*

Well thank you, Jo. I hope that wasn't too much trouble. Doing your nails? Getting a facial? And how is La Stupenda Immaculada? Has she recovered yet?

JO. Recovered?

MRS. WYLIE. You said on the telephone she was upset. Her husband...?

JO. Oh. Right.

MRS. WYLIE. Which frankly didn't surprise me at all the way they carried on. I was fully expecting one of them to pull a knife.

(No response.)

Is she feeling better? Jo?

JO. Hm?

MRS. WYLIE. Is she feeling better?

JO. Ma'am. She's dead.

(Pause.)

MRS. WYLIE. Well I'm not surprised. It must really take it out of you having your husband just walk out the door –

JO. Ma'am –

MRS. WYLIE. Of course it doesn't have to be the best performance she ever gave. Just shove her on stage at this point –

JO. *Ma'am.*

MRS. WYLIE. Jo?

JO. She's dead. I mean she…she's dead. She killed herself.

(*Long pause.*)

MRS. WYLIE. Who?

JO. Elena.

MRS. WYLIE. Firenzi?

JO. (*Nodding, choked up.*) She's in the bedroom.

> (**MRS. WYLIE** *eyes* **JO**, *then walks to the connecting door.*)

MRS. WYLIE. Is this a joke?

JO. (*A sob.*) No.

> (**MRS. WYLIE** *opens the door and steps inside.* **JO** *follows her.* **MRS. WYLIE** *looks at* **ELENA**. *She walks to the bed and pauses. She shakes* **ELENA**'s *shoulder, no response. Gingerly, she opens one of* **ELENA**'s *eyelids.*)

MRS. WYLIE. Jesus Christ.

JO. I know.

MRS. WYLIE. What happened?

JO. She-she got upset. About her husband. She took the whole bottle.

MRS. WYLIE. Jesus Christ!

JO. She left a note –

> (**MRS. WYLIE** *snatches the note from* **JO**.)

I-I-I knew she was upset – she got so excited. I-I mean she grabbed a fork and said she'd kill herself, but then she-she calmed down and she just-just wanted to rest –

MRS. WYLIE. *(Squinting at the note.)* "The fur is gone"?

JO. *(Looking.)* "Fun. The fun is gone and now so am I."

MRS. WYLIE. Oh my God.

JO. I-I thought she was exaggerating.

MRS. WYLIE. They'll crucify me.

JO. It's not your fault.

MRS. WYLIE. They'll want their money back!

>   *(Beat.)*

Lousy tramp. I knew she'd get me.

>   *(To* **ELENA***.)* Are you satisfied, missy!

JO. Ma'am –

MRS. WYLIE. *(Climbing on to the bed and shaking* **ELENA** *violently in a rage.)* ARE YOU PROUD OF YOURSELF??!! FEEL BETTER NOW??!!

JO. *(Trying to pull* **MRS. WYLIE** *off.)* Mrs. Wylie!

MRS. WYLIE. Why me? She could have waited until tomorrow. She could have jumped out of the window after breakfast.

JO. We sang a duet together. I mean I-I really liked her.

>   *(***MRS. WYLIE** *climbs off the bed.)*

MRS. WYLIE. *(Bitter.)* Well… I guess that wraps it up. End of the road. Arrivederci.

>   *(Suddenly she attacks the body again.)*

AHHHH!!

JO. MRS. WYLIE.

>   *(***MRS. WYLIE** *stops, stands up, then kicks the bed.* **JO** *covers* **ELENA**, *head and all, with the*

blanket. **MRS. WYLIE** *walks into the sitting room and* **JO** *follows her.)*

MRS. WYLIE. I'll have to make an announcement, of course. "Ladies and gentlemen – Miss Elena Firenzi killed herself this afternoon, thereby depriving many of us...of a great pleasure. It was universally acknowledged that she sang like an angel, but apparently she wanted to prove it. In short, our star for the evening has departed this world in a final gesture of selfishness and deceit unrivalled in the history of comic opera!"

JO. I think maybe I should make the announcement.

(**MRS. WYLIE** *runs for the connecting door to get at* **ELENA** *again, but* **JO** *grabs her.)*

MRS. WYLIE. AHHHHHHH!

JO. We-we could still do the performance. I think we should.

MRS. WYLIE. Oh of course. Absolutely. We can prop her up and play a record. Add a few lines about Carmen throwing her back out doing the tarantella, then carry her around the stage on a stretcher!

JO. I-I-I mean the understudy.

MRS. WYLIE. The understudy. Of course! My God, you've solved the whole problem! Skip the announcement, stick a note in the program – "The role of Carmen will be sung by Shawna Rupp." And then if there is anyone still in the audience when she takes her bow, they can stone her to death! The ultimate operatic experience! One thundering orgasm of insane violence! Make *Salome* look like *The Magic Flute.*

JO. Ma'am, I think you ought to calm down.

MRS. WYLIE. Right! Good point! We don't want two dead bodies around here. Just think of the smell. Put everybody at the Gala Buffet right off their shrimp!

JO. Ma'am! Let's just – just sit down for a minute. Okay? Ma'am?

> (**MRS. WYLIE** *is dazed. She sits on the couch and* **JO** *sits next to her.*)

MRS. WYLIE. *(A last lunge;* **JO** *grabs her.)* AHH!

JO. It's not your fault, ma'am. It was just...unlucky, that's all. I mean everybody'll understand.

MRS. WYLIE. Yes. Of course they will. And then they'll fire me and throw me to the wolves.

> *(Pause. The rage is over. Black despair. After several seconds,* **MRS. WYLIE** *smiles. Then she chuckles. Then she breaks into laughter, genuine, if slightly hysterical.)*

JO. What's so funny? Ma'am?

MRS. WYLIE. Ohhh! I was just thinking. They probably wouldn't know the difference. The understudy, Shawna Rupp. Give her some great boobs, lots of makeup. If we didn't tell the audience, they'd think she was Elena Firenzi.

JO. Think so?

> *(She thinks about it, then chuckles.)*

I think you're right.

> *(She starts to laugh, in spite of herself – which sets off* **MRS. WYLIE** *again.)*

They-they probably wouldn't know.

MRS. WYLIE. They'd give her a standing ovation!

JO. Bring down the house!

> *(They both laugh uproariously, out of control.)*

JO. Ohhh...

MRS. WYLIE. Ohhh...

JO. It wouldn't work.

MRS. WYLIE. I know.

JO. I mean the company would know it was her –

MRS. WYLIE. Of course.

JO. And the story would leak out –

MRS. WYLIE. And then the audience would hang me. Yes, I realize that.

JO. If she wasn't in the company, I bet it would work.

MRS. WYLIE. But she is.

JO. Yeah. Too bad.

> (*Long pause. Slowly, a light dawns in* **MRS. WYLIE***'s brain. She rolls it over in her mind, then turns her head and looks at* **JO**. **JO** *sees her and smiles amiably. Then she sees the stony, maniacal look in* **MRS. WYLIE***'s eyes – and suddenly* **JO** *looks nervous.*)

MRS. WYLIE. (*Quietly.*) Jo.

JO. Forget it. It wouldn't work. They'd spot me in ten seconds.

MRS. WYLIE. No they wouldn't.

JO. Hey, stop it. The answer's no.

MRS. WYLIE. Jo –

JO. You're out of your mind. I don't even look like her.

MRS. WYLIE. High heels. Lots of hair...

JO. Hey. We were joking. This is life. It's called reality. Remember that?

MRS. WYLIE. You could do it, Jo. I know you could.

JO. *(Starting to panic.)* Hey. Look. Just-just one second, Okay? I don't speak Italian. I-I-I-I-I-I hardly speak English.

MRS. WYLIE. You wouldn't have to speak Italian. And *Carmen* is in French!

JO. Look-look-just-just-Okay? They'd know. They would know. It's me, Jo.

MRS. WYLIE. No they wouldn't! That's the point! They've never seen her before. They're expecting *her*, not *you*.

JO. Yeah, but-but-but –

MRS. WYLIE. They want to see her, Jo. They want to say they've seen her.

JO. But it's an opera! Four acts!

MRS. WYLIE. You know the part. You admitted it.

JO. I can hum it! In the bathtub!

> *(Ring!)*

MRS. WYLIE. You know every single note, I know you do –

JO. Wrong! There's a few at the end, I-I get mixed up –

MRS. WYLIE. Aha!

> *(Into the phone.)*

Yes?

JO. *(Pacing.)* You're out of your mind!

MRS. WYLIE. Yes, Julia.

JO. I mean you're crazy! Okay? You're nuts!

MRS. WYLIE. *(Into the phone.)* No, Elena is much better. She's fine.

JO. No she isn't. She's dead. She's not fine. Fine is living!

MRS. WYLIE. No! Now Julia, just listen. Don't come up. No. Just stay downstairs. Well, frankly, she's still a bit upset about her husband and I think it's better if we meet you backstage.

JO. That's better. That is better. Because she's dead!

MRS. WYLIE. Yes, just Jo. Right. Fine. See you there.

> *(She hangs up.)*

JO. That was a mistake.

MRS. WYLIE. Jo –

JO. No.

MRS. WYLIE. I'm begging you, Jo.

> *(She is.)*

JO. No!

MRS. WYLIE. Look at me, Jo. You can do it. Believe me!

JO. I can't!

MRS. WYLIE. A thousand people! They're getting dressed now. They've got tickets at fifty dollars each, Jo. That's fifty thousand dollars!

JO. Ma'am –

MRS. WYLIE. My whole career! My life, Jo. My children. It's all in your hands.

> *(**MRS. WYLIE** grabs **JO** around the knees and sobs. She looks up – no reaction. She sobs harder.)*

JO. Ohhhh crap!

MRS. WYLIE. I'll never forget this, Jo.

JO. I bet.

> (**MRS. WYLIE** *jumps to her feet and races into
> the bedroom.* **JO**, *now speechless with fear,
> follows her. During the following* **MRS. WYLIE**
> *takes one of the suitcases from the closet and
> puts it on the bed next to* **ELENA**'s *body.*)

MRS. WYLIE. I have it all figured out. It's simple. You
change here into the costume, make-up, padding, the
works. Then we drive to the theatre just in time and
suddenly, bang, you're onstage.

JO. Oh God.

MRS. WYLIE. Between the acts, you'll stay in your dressing
room. Locked up. Then, after it's over, it's straight to
the car, drive back and we're finished.

JO. What about, uh...

> (*She nods at* **ELENA**.)

MRS. WYLIE. No problem. Tomorrow morning we break
the news. She took the pills after the performance and
passed away quietly during the night. This is it.

> (**MRS. WYLIE** *rummages through the suitcase
> and pulls out her costume.*)

This is it. Dress – wig – mantilla –

> (*A knock at the front door and they both
> freeze.*)

Who's that?

JO. How should I know?

MRS. WYLIE. I'll take care of it. You just change and make
it fast.

> (*She hands* **JO** *the suitcase and heads for the
> sitting room.*)

JO. Ma'am?

MRS. WYLIE. Yes, Jo?

JO. Wish me luck.

MRS. WYLIE. We don't need luck, Jo.

JO. Thanks.

> (**MRS. WYLIE** *closes the door.*)

MRS. WYLIE. We need a miracle.

> (*As* **MRS. WYLIE** *heads for the front door,* **JO** *disappears into the bathroom.*)

Who is it?

JULIA. *(Offstage.)* It's me, Lucy. Open the door.

MRS. WYLIE. Julia! I told you not to come up!

JULIA. *(Offstage.)* Open the door, Lucy!

> (**MRS. WYLIE** *opens the door.* **JULIA** *enters. She's about sixty and wears a silver dress covered in sequins. She strikes a pose.*)

How do I look? The truth.

MRS. WYLIE. Like the Chrysler Building.

JULIA. I knew you'd like it.

> (*She sweeps in and twirls around.*)

It's straight from Paris. Haute couture. I feel like one of those fancy French tarts.

MRS. WYLIE. Julia, for God's sake –

JULIA. Now don't be cross, Lucy. I couldn't bear waiting backstage anymore. Not with those shrimp. I could hardly breathe. Besides, I thought I might cheer her up. Suddenly before she knows it she'll feel vital again. Totally alive.

MRS. WYLIE. No, I don't think so.

JULIA. You know what this reminds me of? That opera, the one with the snow falling, and everybody's hungry all the time.

MRS. WYLIE. Julia, please! Just *listen*!

JULIA. I'm listening, Lucy.

MRS. WYLIE. I want you to go to the theatre. Now. All right? As a favor to me.

JULIA. Oh, Lucy. You know how much I admire you.

MRS. WYLIE. *(Moving her toward the door.)* Good. Off you go –

JULIA. But it's just so silly. I'm here already.

MRS. WYLIE. But you won't be soon. You'll be at the theatre.

JULIA. Not if I'm here. I can't be in two places.

MRS. WYLIE. You won't be in two places. You won't be here.

JULIA. Why not?

MRS. WYLIE. Because you'll be there.

JULIA. But why bother? I'm already here –

MRS. WYLIE. Julia, please –!

> *(A knock at the door.)*

Now what?!

JULIA. *(Sitting.)* I think it's the door.

> *(**MRS. WYLIE** stops halfway to the door, returns to just behind **JULIA** and raises her hands as though she's going to strangle her. Then she turns back to the door.)*

MRS. WYLIE. Who is it?!

BELLHOP. *(Offstage.)* Room service. Coffee for two.

MRS. WYLIE. We didn't order any coffee.

BELLHOP. *(Offstage.)* You did so! Ask Jo!

MRS. WYLIE. Well it's cancelled!

JULIA. *(Going to the door.)* Oh stop it, Lucy. You can't just let her stand there.

MRS. WYLIE. Don't –!

> *(She opens the door. The* **BELLHOP** *enters, holding a tray with a coffee service on it. She also has a camera, hanging around her neck. She leaves the door open.)*

BELLHOP. Thank you, madam. You're very kind. That's one out of two.

JULIA. On the table, please.

MRS. WYLIE. And then get out.

JULIA. She's only doing her job, Lucy.

MRS. WYLIE. Well she can do it somewhere else.

BELLHOP. She's not very friendly, is she?

MRS. WYLIE. You, get out! Julia, you too! You promised!

JULIA. I wonder what's keeping Miss Firenzi?

BELLHOP. Is she getting dressed?

JULIA. Apparently.

BELLHOP. *(Going to the connecting door.)* Perhaps she needs some help with her zippers. You know these opera stars, they're helpless –

MRS. WYLIE. STOP!

> *(The* **BELLHOP** *stops, her hand on the doorknob.)*

Take one step into that room and I will *kill* you.

BELLHOP. Fair enough. I'll wait out here.

MRS. WYLIE. You're not waiting any place, you're getting out!

BELLHOP. Fine. As soon as I meet her.

MRS. WYLIE. You're not meeting her.

BELLHOP. Jo promised. That's why I brought the coffee. I'm a bellhop, not a waitress.

MRS. WYLIE. Listen, you –!

> *(In a burst of anger, **MRS. WYLIE** grabs the **BELLHOP** by her shirtfront and hoists her to her feet. Simultaneously, **JERRY** appears at the front door dressed for the evening. He carries a single red rose.)*

JULIA. Lucy!

BELLHOP. Help!

JERRY. *(Rushing in.)* Mother?!

BELLHOP. Help!

JERRY. What are you doing?!

MRS. WYLIE. *(To the **BELLHOP**.)* Are you getting out?!

BELLHOP. I'm getting wrinkled.

JERRY. Mother, stop it! What's the matter?!

> *(**MRS. WYLIE** drops the **BELLHOP**.)*

BELLHOP. *(Smoothing herself out.)* We had a slight misunderstanding. Then she went insane.

MRS. WYLIE. *(To **JERRY**.)* What the hell are you doing here?

JERRY. I came to see Miss Firenzi. To wish her luck.

MRS. WYLIE. Well you're not going to, so get out!

JERRY.   Mother, what's the matter with you? Has something happened?

MRS. WYLIE.   *(After a slight pause.)* No.

JULIA.   She's been under a lot of strain lately. Haven't you, Lucy?

MRS. WYLIE.   No!

BELLHOP.   Yes you have, Lucy, I can tell.

MRS. WYLIE.   Get her out of here, I'm warning you –

JERRY.   This isn't like her at all.

BELLHOP.   Oh yes it is.

MRS. WYLIE.   Get out! Now!

BELLHOP.   All right!

> *(With dignity.)*

I will be happy to leave –

JULIA.   *(To* **MRS. WYLIE.***)* There.

BELLHOP.   As soon as I get one picture.

MRS. WYLIE.   Give me the camera.

BELLHOP.   No.

MRS. WYLIE.   *(Advancing.)* Hand it over, you little twit!

BELLHOP.   *(Retreating.)* Stay away from me!

> **(MRS. WYLIE** *chases the* **BELLHOP** *around the sofa, with* **JERRY** *and* **JULIA** *chasing* **MRS. WYLIE.***)*

JERRY.   Mother!

JULIA.   Lucy!

BELLHOP.   Hold it! Click.

(The **BELLHOP** *snaps a picture of the other three, who pose momentarily without realizing it. Then, immediately the chase resumes.)*

MRS. WYLIE. I want the camera!

(As the chase continues in the sitting room, the bathroom door opens and **JO** *emerges, dressed head to toe as Carmen, in a colorful, sexy costume with a distinctive dark wig, big bust, high heels, a lot of eye makeup as well as a veil and a mantilla. She wears her glasses over the veil.)*

(She staggers into the bedroom, visibly quaking. She makes it to the connecting door and puts her ear against it. The action in the sitting room has continued without a break.)

JULIA. Lucy!

BELLHOP. Help!

MRS. WYLIE. Get the camera! Jerry!

JULIA. Lucy, let her take the picture.

BELLHOP. Lucy, stop it!

*(***JO** *raps sharply on the connecting door. The others freeze and turn to the noise.)*

JULIA. It's her!

JERRY. She must be ready.

JULIA. *(Calling.)* Signora Firenzi? Is that you?

JO. *(From the bedroom.)* ...Ciao.

MRS. WYLIE. Jesus Christ.

JULIA. *(Calling.)* We're all waiting for you.

JO. *(Heavy accent.)* Pleese. Send a-me in a-da room, a-Mrs. a-Wylie.

JULIA. What a beautiful accent.

JERRY. *(Nudging her.)* Mother…

MRS. WYLIE. I heard her, thank you.

JULIA. *(Calling.)* She'll be right in!

MRS. WYLIE. Julia. Jerry. I'm asking you one last time to leave the room.

JERRY. But I've got to talk to her!

MRS. WYLIE. Jerry –

JERRY. It's important!

JULIA. Oh, Lucy, don't be such a pill. She has to meet us some time.

JERRY. Exactly.

JULIA. *(To* **JERRY.***)* Now don't you worry. You're staying right here. And so am I.

JO. *(From the bedroom.)* 'Allo?

JULIA. Lucy. Go inside!

MRS. WYLIE. You're going to regret this, Julia.

JULIA. You always say that and I never do.

JO. 'Allo?!

MRS. WYLIE. I'm coming!

> *(She goes to the connecting door and turns the knob.)*

It's me.

> *(***JO*** hides behind the door as* ***MRS. WYLIE*** *backs into the bedroom, shielding it from the others. She closes the door – then sees* ***JO*** *and jumps backward.)*

Good God!

> (**JULIA**, **JERRY**, *and the* **BELLHOP** *are by this time listening at the door, straining to hear what's happening.*)

JO. I can't do it!

MRS. WYLIE. Keep it down!

JO. *(Whispering.)* I can't do it!

MRS. WYLIE. Jo. You look marvelous!

JO. You're crazy!

MRS. WYLIE. You'll be wonderful.

JO. No I won't. Believe me.

JULIA. *(In the sitting room, to* **JERRY***.)* Oh no! It's awful!

JERRY. What's the matter?

JULIA. I can't hear a thing.

MRS. WYLIE. You'll get a curtain call just for the costume.

JO. Fine. Then you wear it!

MRS. WYLIE. Jo, we have a bargain. You promised.

JO. I know. I'm sorry. I'll-I'll-I'll make it up to you. I'll pay you money. Big money.

MRS. WYLIE. Now just relax! Sit down! You're wound up over nothing.

JO. Nothing…

MRS. WYLIE. Think of it, Jo. There you'll be. Standing on stage and looking radiant. In the background, the peasants are starving and singing quietly. Then the spotlight hits you and wham! You're bathed in light. Your face, your neck, your…

> *(Looks at* **JO**'*s large fake bust.)*

MRS. WYLIE. legs, You look breathtaking! Then you start singing, the Habanera, and your voice, alone, fills the theatre to the second balcony. No one breathes.

JO. Including me. That's the trouble.

MRS. WYLIE. You can do it, Jo.

JO. I can't.

MRS. WYLIE. It's your big break. Everything you've ever dreamed about –

JO. I can't even walk! I-I-I'm shaking all over! I'm losing weight!

MRS. WYLIE. Jo –

JO. Please! I'll do anything else! I promise!

MRS. WYLIE. Jo, get a hold of yourself!

JO. *(Near tears.)* You don't understand! *I can't do it! I can't, I can't! I'm nobody!* ...I'm sorry.

> *(Pause.* **MRS. WYLIE** *realizes that it's no use. She sighs heavily. She's done all she can.)*

MRS. WYLIE. All right, Jo. Go change. I'll make an announcement. I suppose it wouldn't have worked anyway.

> *(***MRS. WYLIE** *steels herself, grimly, and leaves the bedroom, closing the door behind her.* **JO** *remains where she is and doesn't move.)*

JULIA. Well?!

JERRY. Where is she?!

BELLHOP. What happened?

MRS. WYLIE. Please. I have a short announcement to make. Miss Firenzi has been under a great deal of strain lately. Indeed as some of you know, today was not one of her better days.

JULIA. Lucy!

JERRY. What's the matter?!

JULIA. Is she sick?!

MRS. WYLIE. Miss Firenzi is unexpectedly ill. She will not be singing in this evening's performance.

JULIA. Lucy, you must be joking!

MRS. WYLIE. I'm afraid not.

JULIA. Oh my God! Lucy, do something!

MRS. WYLIE. There's nothing I can do.

JULIA. Oh good God!

JERRY. It's my fault. It's all my fault.

MRS. WYLIE. Jerry –

JERRY. It is!

JULIA. Lucy, talk to her! Tell her it's too late to get sick! Say something!

MRS. WYLIE. I tried, believe me.

> *(Without warning, **JERRY** bolts toward the bedroom.)*

JERRY. Miss Firenzi!

MRS. WYLIE. Jerry!

> *(Too late. He swings the door open. **JO** sees **JERRY** and bounds to the door. To prevent him from seeing **ELENA**'s body, she advances into the sitting room, pulling off her glasses as she goes and closes the connecting door behind her.)*

JERRY. Please! I've got to talk to you!

> *(**JO** is speechless, so are the others.)*

JERRY. Miss Firenzi, I-I know you've had a bad day, and you aren't feeling well. And I'm sure you don't feel like singing tonight, after what happened. But the thing is, everybody's counting on you. I mean, they've all been waiting, for months, and-and looking forward to it. And it really won't matter if it isn't your very best, I mean just so it's you. And I know it's asking a lot, but if you *could* do it, even the first act, we'd all be so grateful. So could you? Please?

>   (**JO** *is stunned. She looks at* **JERRY**, *then at* **MRS. WYLIE**, *then back at* **JERRY**. *Pause.*)

JO. *(Shrugging: accent.)* Sure. Why not, eh?

>   (*All hell breaks loose.*)

JERRY.	**JULIA.**	**BELLHOP.**
Oh thank you so much! You have no idea how much this means to me. I mean, I know it'll be a strain after what happened –	Oh, Miss Firenzi, on behalf of the Opera Guild, I want to thank you, from the bottom of my heart, for your courage and – and sacrifice –	What a woman. Miss Firenzi, my name is Beverly and I've always wanted to meet you since I was this high and I'm so impressed with you!

MRS. WYLIE. HOLD IT!

>   (*They fall silent.*)

If we don't leave immediately, she'll miss the curtain.

BELLHOP. Oh my God. I've got to change! I'll see you there!

>   (*She exits running.*)

MRS. WYLIE. Julia. Shall we go?

JULIA. Yes, of course. I fly on wings of song.

>   *(She exits.)*

MRS. WYLIE. Gerald?

JERRY. I'm coming, Mother.

>   **(MRS. WYLIE** *exits.* **JO** *turns away, but* **JERRY** *hasn't left yet.)*

Oh, Miss Firenzi, I've got to talk to you!

JO. Huh? Hey. We talk later, eh? I, uh, got to prepare myself –

JERRY. It's about your husband. I did something terrible!

JO. A-Gerald. A-please.

>   *(Pause.)*

There are some few moments when we done look back, and we done look ahead. And for that a-one moment, we have a-music, we have a-happiness, we have a-hope. Eh? That's all.

>   **(JERRY** *hands her the rose he brought with him.)*

JERRY. This is for you.

JO. *(Accepting it.)* Grazie.

>   *(He extends his hand to shake.* **JO** *takes his hand, holds it for a moment, then lifts it to her cheek and holds it there.* **JERRY** *is breathless. Then he reels out of the room light-headed.)*

>   **(JO** *watches him exit. She's stunned. Then she falls to her knees sobbing with fear. In the process, she drops the rose.)*

(After a moment, she hears [and we hear] two voices – her own and Elena's – singing the final moments of the Gioconda *duet that they sang in Scene One. The music grows louder and swells in beauty.* **JO** *listens to it; then sees the rose and picks it up and smells it. Her courage grows. She gets to her feet and stands up straight and tall. As the music continues,* **JO** *turns majestically and walks to the corridor door, arms out, her dress trailing behind her. At the threshold, she pauses and turns back. She comes to the footlights, acknowledges the thundering applause in her head, throws a kiss to the audience, and then turns again and hurries out of the door to her debut.)*

(At this moment – in the bedroom – the covers on the bed move, and **ELENA** *sits up with an effort, pulling the covers from her face. Groggy and heavily drugged, she looks around, as…)*

(The curtain falls.)

ACT TWO

Scene One

*(Later that night, about eleven p.m. There is one striking difference from the last time we saw the suite: the bed is empty and **ELENA** is gone. In addition, the bathroom and connecting doors are both ajar, and the front door is in the closed position, but not pulled shut.)*

(In the darkness, we hear the final moments of Carmen, *as Don José sings "O Carmen, Carmen!" the orchestra plays the final chords, and we hear the audience at the opera house go wild. Then the lights come up, and we hear someone knocking at the front door.)*

JERRY. *(Offstage.)* It's open.

JULIA. *(Offstage.)* That's odd.

*(**JULIA** and **JERRY** enter, cautiously at first. Both are dressed as in the previous scene.)*

Elena...?

JERRY. *(Calling.)* Miss Firenzi?

JULIA. *(Into the bedroom.)* Elena?

JERRY. I guess she's not back yet.

JULIA. Apparently not.

*(**JULIA** pulls the connecting door closed.)*

JERRY. Oh my God. She was ethereal!

JULIA. Ethereal isn't the word, my dear. She was box office all the way.

(Ring!)

I wonder who that could be.

JERRY. Maybe it's her.

JULIA. *(Into the phone.)* Hello? ...No she isn't back yet, I'm afraid. Who is this, please?

(Startled.)

Oh my goodness. Is anything... Julia Leverett. Chairwoman of the Opera Guild.

JERRY. Who is it?

JULIA. The police.

JERRY. Police?

JULIA. Is anything wrong, officer? ...Yes, I was there.

JERRY. What's the matter?

JULIA. Shh! ...Oh dear. I see... Well that's good... Oh dear! ...Oh good... Oh dear... I certainly will. Thank you very much. Goodbye.

JERRY. Well?

JULIA. It's very sad actually. Apparently some lunatic dressed as Carmen tried to get into the theatre tonight. She said she was Elena Firenzi.

JERRY. Oh no.

JULIA. When they wouldn't let her in, she started screaming in Italian, so the stage manager called the police.

JERRY. Did they get her?

JULIA. Well, they arrested her and dragged her off, but she got away down an alley. Apparently the poor woman's demented. When they grabbed her, she actually hit a policeman.

JERRY. Oh God.

JULIA. They're sending two of their men over to keep an eye out.

JERRY. I hope nothing happens.

JULIA. That's all we need at the reception is some lunatic on the rampage. We'll have enough of those already when the Board starts drinking. I suppose we'd better go. They'll start arriving any minute now.

JERRY. Maybe I should wait here. I could tell her that you're looking for her. Just trying to help.

JULIA. Of course you are. And I won't tell Jo if you don't.

JERRY. Jo? Oh, please. She won't care. She didn't even show up tonight.

JULIA. *(Teasing.)* If I see her downstairs, shall I tell her you're looking for her?

JERRY. No thank you.

JULIA. How about Elena?

JERRY. No…

JULIA. Do you know that *Time* magazine has called her the sexiest woman alive.

JERRY. Why would I care?

JULIA. Oh, pul-lease.

JERRY. Aunt Julia!

JULIA. See you later, my dear.

> *(**JULIA** exits, closing the door behind her.
> **JERRY** goes to the telephone and clicks for the
> operator.)*

JERRY. *(Into the phone.)* Stage door of the Opera House, please... Hello, Harry? It's Jerry Wylie... Just fine. How are you? ...Yes it was. It was terrific. Hey, I was wondering, is...is Jo around backstage by any chance?

> *(Disappointed.)*

Oh not at all? ...No, that's all right. It's nothing special.

> *(We hear the sound of the front door being unlocked. Hurried:)*

Thanks, Harry. Bye.

> *(He hangs up. The door opens and **JO** enters. She's still in full costume and make-up. She doesn't see **JERRY** at first.)*

Hi.

> *(**JO** is startled.)*

JO. Ciao.

> *(**JO** hesitates...then finds her courage and sashays into the room, full of confidence. She is all woman. **JERRY** is suddenly nervous, being alone with "Elena." And he's very aware of how sexy she is. He tries to make conversation, but **JO** isn't helping.)*

JERRY. I-I hope you don't mind me being here. The door was open but you weren't here. Which I guess you know, since you were somewhere else. Wanh! So then I waited for you, because I have a message from Aunt Julia. She's not really my aunt, you know. I just call her my aunt since my mother never had any sisters. In case you're wondering. Anyway, she asked me to-to wait here and remind you that she hopes you'll make a speech at the reception. In English. I mean, not Italian because they probably don't...speak Italian. Anyway, and I'm sure they'd really appreciate it, if you feel like it, which you probably don't, which is understandable, and that's the message.

JO. Thanks. That's a-very nice of you, eh? To give a-me the massage.

> *(She realizes her mistake with the word and turns away rolling her eyes.)*

JERRY. It was nothing really.

JO. It's a-very sweet.

JERRY. ...So. I guess I ought to be going.

JO. Yeah? That's a-too bad.

JERRY. It is?

JO. Yeah. For me, eh?

JERRY. Oh. Well. I don't *have* to go. If you don't think so. I mean it's your bedroom. Suite. Rooms. Of course, I'm sure you'd like to just relax a little now so I can take off your clothes. You! Do your own clothes. Off. Change your clothes, into something more comfortable. So I probably shouldn't be here for that. If you don't think so.

JO. Hey. I'm gonna tell you something, it's gonna shock a-you, eh?

JERRY. Oh come on.

JO. It's gonna be a big a-surprise. Okay?

JERRY. Okay.

JO. Tonight, when I'm a-singin' my love song to Don José, I'm a-thinkin' of you.

JERRY. Me?

JO. *"Tout doux, Monsieur, tout doux. / Je vais danser en votre honneur, / et vous verrez, seigneur, / comment je sais moi-même accompagner ma danse!"* "Tonight I will dance in your honor in this dark a-place, and you will make love to me as the bugle sounds, to a-celebrate our immense a-love."

JERRY. ...Me?

> (*She kisses him on the lips. He responds. We hear fireworks in the distance.* **JERRY** *breaks and looks up, then grabs* **JO** *in a kiss of passion. They both feel breathless and hot. They're kissing and kissing.*)

But what about your husband?

JO. My husband? ...Oh my *husband*. That husband.

JERRY. Pasquale.

JO. Pasquale. He's...he's uh... Heh. This is gonna surprise you, eh?

> (*Grave.*)

He's not a-my husband.

JERRY. He's not?

JO. No. He pretends he's a-my husband. He likes to think so, eh? It's a-very sad.

JERRY. Elena!

> (*They go at it again, with even more enthusiasm, both of them getting hotter by the second. Without warning, there's a knock at the door.*)

Oh hell!

> (**JERRY** *faces front and we see now that his hair is askew and his face is smudged with her lipstick and rouge.*)

MRS. WYLIE. (*Bang bang bang; Offstage.*) Open up.

JERRY. It's my mother, dammit!

(He hurries to the mirror to compose himself, and sees his face and screams.)

JO. *(Buying time.)* Who's the-ere?

MRS. WYLIE. *(Offstage.)* It's me.

JO. Who is "me," please?

MRS. WYLIE. Who do you think it is? Now open the door!

JO. Ciao.

> *(**MRS. WYLIE** enters carrying a distinctive opening night dress for **JO** on a hanger.)*

MRS. WYLIE. Where have you been?! I've been looking all over for – Gerald!

JERRY. Hello, Mother.

MRS. WYLIE. What are you doing here?

JERRY. I'm here to give Miss Firenzi a message.

MRS. WYLIE. Oh. Oh I see. Miss Firenzi.

JERRY. Aunt Julia wants her to speak at the reception.

MRS. WYLIE. Well, we'll have to see about that, now won't we. I'm sure that Miss Firenzi is awfully tired... Aren't you?

JO. Hm? Yeah. Sure.

(She yawns.)

JERRY. Well, I guess I ought to be going then.

MRS. WYLIE. What a good idea.

JERRY. It was nice meeting you, Miss Firenzi. I hope to see you again some time.

JO. Me too, eh?

JERRY. *Soon.*

JO. Soon?

JERRY. *(Nodding hard at the door.)* You certainly *unlocked* the door to our hearts this evening.

JO. Thanks.

JERRY. And will again, I'm sure.

JO. *(Not getting it.)* I hope a-so, eh?

JERRY. So I won't even say goodbye. Just arrivederci.

JO. Ciao.

> (**JERRY** *exits.* **JO** *closes the door; in her own voice:)*

Well?

MRS. WYLIE. Jo, Jo, Jo. Haha! We did it!

JO. We?

MRS. WYLIE. What a triumph! Jo, you had them in the palm of your hand. They ached for you, Jo. They longed for you.

JO. I guess I was all right then.

MRS. WYLIE. Let me put it this way, Jo. I owe you one.

JO. No you don't. You owe me several.

MRS. WYLIE. You're right. I do. And if there's any little favor you can think of, Jo, any trifling thing –

JO. Next season.

MRS. WYLIE. Hm?

JO. I thought I'd start out next season with *Tosca*.

MRS. WYLIE. Oh.

JO. Then Mimi in *La Bohème*, then finish off with something lighter, like *Die Fledermaus*.

MRS. WYLIE. Jo –

JO. Ma'am?

MRS. WYLIE. It just so happens, I have another idea. It's an inspiration. A flash of genius!

JO. What?

MRS. WYLIE. Verdi's *Requiem*.

JO. I don't get it.

MRS. WYLIE. Requiem! Mass for the dead. Who is dead, Jo?

JO. Elena! I almost forgot.

MRS. WYLIE. Well I didn't, and I have it all figured out. Tomorrow morning we arrive together. We knock at the door, no answer, so we get the manager. She lets us in and "Oh-my-God, the woman is dead! Elena! Elena! What have you done?" Too late. She's gone. Too bad. Now within the hour, it hits the wire service and by Monday we've got every newspaper and magazine in the country here. So – I call a press conference. I wear basic black with my Tiffany choker. "We, of the Cleveland Grand Opera Company, we who were graced by the final warblings of that immortal soprano which is no more, we will honor the memory of La Stupenda a week from today at eight o'clock with a single performance of Miss Firenzi's favourite and sadly appropriate work of music, Verdi's *Requiem*."

JO. Was that her favorite?

MRS. WYLIE. How the hell should I know?

JO. Sorry.

MRS. WYLIE. The point is, my dear, it'll put us on the map! The publicity will be tremendous. I couldn't have planned the whole thing better if I'd strangled her myself. Now guess, Jo, guess who will sing the soprano solos in the *Requiem*. Hm?

JO. Me?

MRS. WYLIE. You.

JO. Thanks.

MRS. WYLIE. Now listen, I've got to get downstairs to the big reception, so here's the drill. Put this on,

(The gown.)

and turn back into Jo. Then wait in here, with the door locked, and do not, under any circumstances, let anyone in. I'll make Elena's excuses downstairs, and then when the reception's over, I'll come back up and we'll both go celebrate. All right? Good. Now go change.

(She heads for the door.)

JO. Uh, ma'am?

MRS. WYLIE. Jo?

JO. I, uh, I just want to say that I-I really liked her, and I don't think you ever quite realized what a...a really beautiful person she was. I mean, before she died.

MRS. WYLIE. Jo. Believe me. I loved her like a sister. But there's nothing we can do for her now. It's just too late.

JO. I guess so.

MRS. WYLIE. If it's any comfort to you, Jo, just remember – from here on out, it's clear sailing. Absolutely nothing can go wrong.

> (**MRS. WYLIE** *exits, closing the door behind her. Simultaneously, the bedroom/corridor door bursts open and* **ELENA** *enters. She, too, is dressed as Carmen, in exactly the same costume and make-up that* **JO** *is wearing.)*
>
> (**ELENA** *is in a state of panic. Exhausted and bedraggled, she pants heavily from running. Her eyes dart madly in every direction as she leans against the door, gasping for air.)*

(Simultaneously, a siren wails from the street below as though a police car is pulling up at the hotel. JO walks to the window and looks down. ELENA hears the siren and dives into the closet, closing the door behind her. JO shrugs and heads for the bedroom, carrying the gown. As she reaches the connecting door, she hesitates and braces herself.)

JO. Poor Elena.

(She sighs, covers her eyes, and enters the room, heading for the bathroom. JO doesn't want to see Elena's body – she couldn't bear it. And yet, she can't help herself. She separates her fingers and glances at the bed; then covers her eyes again and turns away. Poor Elena! She continues into the bathroom and closes the door. Then, from the bathroom:)

Oh my God!

(JO runs out of the bathroom [without the gown] and stares at the bed, dumbfounded. She tears away the covers, looks under the bed and around the room. No Elena!)

Oh my God!

(She runs out of the bedroom into the corridor, closing the door behind her.)

MRS. WYLIE!

(Beat. Slowly the closet door opens and ELENA emerges. She looks around and listens. Not a sound. She sighs heavily, then totters cautiously through the bedroom and into the sitting room. She looks around the room. She feels certain now that she's safe at last and sinks onto the sofa and closes her eyes. At

which point, **JULIA** *enters through the front door and sees* **ELENA** *from the back, sitting quietly on the sofa. She smiles; then walks silently into the room and covers her eyes with her hands.)*

JULIA. Guess who?

ELENA. AHH!

JULIA. Now aren't you ashamed of yourself. Sitting here quietly enjoying yourself, while everyone downstairs is simply dying to meet you.

ELENA. Excuse me signora, but who are you?

JULIA. You're angry with me, aren't you?

ELENA. Angry?

JULIA. Here I am, haranguing you about the reception when I haven't even told you how magnificent you were tonight. Elena. My darling woman. How can I ever thank you?

ELENA. For what?

JULIA. For what? For what you did this evening!

ELENA. I did nothing, I swear! It wasn't me!

JULIA. No it wasn't you. You're right. It was Carmen. There, onstage, in flesh and blood. It was passion and it was life. It was lust and it was pain. And as I sat there in the theatre tonight, hanging on your every note, I thought to myself: Now at this moment, I am hearing the greatest performance of any opera star who has ever lived!

ELENA. ...I was good, eh?

JULIA. Words cannot express it.

ELENA. I think I'm a-gonna sit down, okay?

JULIA. You poor thing. You've had a bad day, haven't you?

ELENA. I have.

JULIA. Of course you have, and you've been very brave. But, Elena, dear Elena, you will come down to the reception, won't you? For just a few minutes?

ELENA. No, I'm a-gonna excuse.

JULIA. But, Elena, you promised me!

ELENA. I did?

JULIA. Elena Firenzi. I'm surprised at you. How could you possibly disappoint me like this. Me. Julia.

ELENA. I'm a-so sorry, eh?

JULIA. And I'm sorry, too. For I simply will not take no for an answer. I will not budge from this spot until you agree.

(She folds her arms and stands firm.)

There are times, I'm afraid, when the iron foot must be placed firmly in the velvet sock, and only then, with one swift kick, can we put the bird in flight.

ELENA. ...Okay, I give up.

JULIA. You do?

ELENA. Yeah.

JULIA. Oh, Elena, you're wonderful! I knew you wouldn't let us down. Let's go!

ELENA. No. Hey...

(She turns on the charm and takes her hand.)

Julia, I'm a-tired, eh? I need a few minutes to uh, get off-a my shoes and wash a-my face. Okay? Julia...

JULIA. Oh my dearest Elena. You've made me so very happy. Is there anything I can do for you?

ELENA. Yeah. Go.

JULIA. I understand. Poor darling. You need some time alone.

(At the front door.)

Every minute shall seem an hour, and every hour a second. And so I fly.

(She exits, closing the door.)

ELENA. Jesus Christ!

(She thinks for a moment about what to do – then springs into action. She rushes into the bedroom, grabs her suitcase, and puts it on the bed to pack. Then a thought strikes her.)

Train station.

(She hurries into the sitting room to get the phone book.)

Train, train, train.

*(She finds the phone book and riffles through it searching for "train station." At which moment, the front door opens and **LEO** enters.)*

(He looks gorgeous. His clothes are expensive and casual in just the right way, and somehow they let us know exactly what's underneath them.)

*(By this time, **ELENA** has found the appropriate page and scans the column.)*

Tractors. Trailers. Trophies –

LEO. 'Allo dere.

*(**ELENA** sees him, gasps, and drops the phone book.)*

Are you surprised to see me zo zoon?

ELENA. You could a-say that, ya.

LEO. Ha ha ha! I like der surprises. Zo perhaps ve relax now and have der champagne. Vhat do you t'ink?

ELENA. That sounds a-lovely.

LEO. May I use der phone?

> (**LEO** *walks to the telephone.* **ELENA** *watches him, fascinated. He picks up the phone and clicks for the operator.*)

Room zervice, please.

> (*As he waits, he smiles at* **ELENA**. *She smiles back. Into the phone.*)

Yes, I'd like to order der bottle of champagne.

(*To* **ELENA***:*) Is Mumm all right?

ELENA. She's a-fine, thank you.

LEO. Mumm is fine. (*Hangs up phone.*) Elena. Can I ask you der very important qvestion?

ELENA. Of course. Hey.

LEO. I vant you to be totally honest mitt me. Okay, you promise?

ELENA. I cross a-my heart.

LEO. Brutal, if necessary.

ELENA. Noo...

LEO. Pleaze!

ELENA. Okay.

> (*Pause.*)

LEO. Vas I good tonight?

ELENA. ...Good?

LEO. Vas I amazing? Vas I out of der park? I'm sure is not zo easy to judge my performance, having done it mitt me only vonce. But vould you say I vas...impressive tonight?

ELENA. *(Trying to work it out.)* We spent a-some time together, eh?

LEO. Ho, ho, ve sure did!

ELENA. Yeah?

LEO. Now I vant der truth. Take der big climax at de end. Ba-boom! Would you say I vas somet'ing special tonight?

ELENA. Special?

LEO. You don't think so?

ELENA. No, I do! I do! I am trying to remember.

LEO. I know I'm only in Cleveland, Elena, but I can take it, believe me. I am very experienced.

ELENA. So I have heard.

LEO. Now you of course vere incredible. You sounded like der screaming goose in der forest, a thing of beauty. How do you do it?!

ELENA. I have no idea.

LEO. But der qvestion I am asking is vas *I* good too. Did I live up to my reputation, did I *dazzle* you?! Did I make you feel somet'ing down in your basement?

ELENA. Basement?

LEO. Did I *move* you?

ELENA. Sure, sure...

LEO. Do you mean dat?

ELENA. Yes.

LEO. And you thought I vas good?

ELENA. Great.

LEO. Really?

ELENA. Like the goose in the forest.

LEO. Oh Elena! Elena! This means zo much to me! Me, Leo "der tulip" Hoffmeier, pleasing Elena Firenzi, it is like der dream of der Vikings in der Valhalla!

ELENA. Hooray.

LEO. Now Elena, tell me. If I vas dat good and I moved you mitt my voice, is it possible, Elena, dat I could meet your agent?

ELENA. My agent?

LEO. Ja. Und I vould not stint, I vould spend hours mitt her. Der screaming goose vould live again! So vhat do you say?!

ELENA. If that's what you want.

LEO. Oh, it is, it is.

ELENA. Then she is all yours.

LEO. Oh, Elena! You make me so happy. How can I thank you?

ELENA. Hey, it's a-my pleasure, eh?

LEO. It is gonna be, I promise you!

> (He pulls off his shirt in a single movement and he is tremendously ripped. Then he takes her in his arms and kisses her, passionately. She kisses him back with equal passion. Almost at once we hear a knock at the front door.)

Now who is *dat? I vas joost gettin' good.*

ELENA. *(She can barely breathe.)* Who is, pleese?

JERRY. *(Offstage.)* It's me. Jerry.

ELENA. *(To* **LEO**, *whispering.)* Who is Jerry?

LEO. Da son of der manager. Big opera fan. Der biggen schmucken. I am guessing he is vanting your autograph.

JERRY. Open up!

ELENA. Minuto!

LEO. Go, you answer und I go inside. I am on der fire and must qvench it qvickly.

ELENA. We will qvench together.

LEO. Good. Keep varm.

> *(He takes his shirt, throws her a kiss, and exits through the bedroom door, closing it behind him.)*

> *(***ELENA*** opens the front door and* ***JERRY*** *hurries in.)*

JERRY. I slipped out during one of the speeches, so I don't think anybody noticed. Of course I might have been going to the men's room or out for a walk, I mean there's nothing wrong with that, except I think I looked suspicious.

ELENA. How do you do.

JERRY. A lot better, now that I'm here. Are you all right?

ELENA. I'm a-fine, thank you.

JERRY. Good.

ELENA. So.

JERRY. So.

ELENA. I think I know why you come, eh?

JERRY. I'm sure you do.

ELENA. You want a-my autograph.

JERRY. Is that what you call it in Italian?

ELENA. In Italian is "autografo."

> (**JERRY** *turns his back on* **ELENA**, *afraid to look at her. During the following he doesn't see what* **ELENA**'s *doing – which is looking around on the tables for a pen and a piece of paper.)*

JERRY. And what's the word for "love" in Italian? "Amore"?

ELENA. *(Searching.)* Hey, that's good. You speak a-the language, eh?

JERRY. I never would have believed this could happen.

ELENA. Life is funny eh?

JERRY. It certainly is.

> (*By now* **ELENA** *has found the pen and paper and sits, facing away from* **JERRY**, *to use the coffee table to write on.)*

ELENA. So. What would you like me to say, eh?

> *(Writing.)*

"Jerry..."

JERRY. Elena...

ELENA. I get to that.

JERRY. *(Still facing away from her.)* Elena, before we go any further, I want you to know that I don't usually do things like this.

ELENA. No?

JERRY. No. Which doesn't mean that I'm not looking forward to it.

ELENA. Hey. I done mind. Honest.

JERRY. *(Pale.)* You "don't mind"?

>   *(They face each other.)*

ELENA. Is not a big deal, eh? I do it all the time.

JERRY. Well. Then maybe we should forget about it.

ELENA. No! Hey. For me is a pleasure. A privilege. It make me feel proud, eh?

JERRY. Do you mean that?

>   *(They turn away from each other again.)*

ELENA. Sure. And I'm gonna make it a-very special. Just a-for you. "Jerry."

JERRY. I *want* it to be special, Elena. For both of us. I want it to be everything we ever dreamed of!

ELENA. Hey. I do my best, okay?

>   *(**JERRY** takes off his jacket. **ELENA** reads:)*

"Jerry."

>   *(Writing.)*

"A very special a-person…"

>   *(**JERRY** takes off his shirt. He's not the Greek God that **LEO** was, but he's pretty impressive.)*

"And a-handsome to look at."

JERRY. Thanks.

>   *(He takes off his trousers.)*

ELENA. *(Signing with a flourish.)* "Firenzi." So now our names are gonna be linked a-forever.

JERRY. Our names? Forever?

ELENA. *(Feeling the paper.)* Should last pretty good.

JERRY. All right. Just hold on tight.

> *(She turns in surprise at the tone of his voice and sees him shirtless in his boxer shorts.)*

ELENA. Yiy!!

JERRY. I'm all yours.

ELENA. Jerry!

JERRY. Elena!

> *(They come together in a passionate embrace, kissing each other all over. Then, without warning, there's a knock on the door. They both freeze.)*

Oh crap! Are you expecting anybody?

ELENA. No.

MRS. WYLIE. *(Offstage.)* Jo?!

ELENA. Jo?

JERRY. Oh hell, it's Mother!

ELENA. Mother?

JERRY. If she finds me like this, she'll go nuts!

ELENA. Nuts?

JERRY. She'll go crazy! I've gotta hide!

MRS. WYLIE. *(Offstage; knocking.)* Jo?!

> *(**JERRY** heads toward the bedroom.)*

ELENA. No!

> *(Too late. **JERRY** opens the door and enters the bedroom. **ELENA** runs in after him.)*

JERRY. Closet or bathroom?

ELENA. Closet!

JERRY. You're right!

(He runs to the closet and opens the door.)

Just say you haven't seen me!

ELENA. You haven't seen me.

(He kisses her quickly, then disappears into the closet, closing the door. At which point, the bathroom door opens and **LEO** *enters. He wears a towel.)*

LEO. Is he gone bye-bye?

ELENA. Not yet.

LEO. Vell tell him to get lost! I am Dutchman! We have der short fuse. Get it?

ELENA. Got it.

LEO. Good. Perhaps I vill run der bath mitt der oils. You vill join me?

ELENA. Oils? I wone be long.

(He exits back into the bathroom, closing the door. **ELENA** *sighs; then runs into the sitting room, closing the connecting door as she goes; then runs to the corridor door and opens it.)*

MRS. WYLIE. *(Offstage – then on.)* JO!

ELENA. Ciao.

*(***MRS. WYLIE** *glares at her and enters.)*

MRS. WYLIE. What are you *doing* in here?!

ELENA. *(Shrugging innocently.)* Nothing.

MRS. WYLIE. You haven't even changed yet.

ELENA. Change?

MRS. WYLIE. I told you to change! For heaven's sake, you'll ruin everything!

ELENA. I'm a-sorry, eh?

(*Trying to get her out.*)

Thanks a-for coming.

MRS. WYLIE. Will you stop with the phony accent! I'm not amused.

ELENA. You done like it?

MRS. WYLIE. Lock. I know you think this is great fun. You're La Stupenda. You're a sex symbol –

ELENA. Yeah.

MRS. WYLIE. But it's not the time to horse around! Just imagine what would happen if anybody found out. My blood runs cold when I even –

(*She stops in her tracks. She's staring at the floor at Jerry's shirt and trousers. She picks them up and holds them out. She looks at* **ELENA.**)

Is there a man in here?

ELENA. Yeah.

MRS. WYLIE. Are you out of your mind?!

ELENA. I'm not so sure.

MRS. WYLIE. You're really having a field day, aren't you?

ELENA. (*Shrugging.*) Heh...

MRS. WYLIE. (*Lowering her voice.*) Can he hear us?

ELENA. I dunno.

MRS. WYLIE. That explains the accent.

ELENA. It does?

    (**MRS. WYLIE** *sidles over to the kitchenette.*)

MRS. WYLIE. *(Whispering.)* Is he in there?

ELENA. No.

MRS. WYLIE. Well where is he?

ELENA. The bathroom.

MRS. WYLIE. The bathroom? Are you crazy? What about the body?

ELENA. The body?

MRS. WYLIE. The body!

ELENA. Like I said, he's in the bathroom.

MRS. WYLIE. Not that body. The other body.

ELENA. Oh.

    (Resigned.) The closet.

MRS. WYLIE. The closet? You stuffed the body in the closet?

ELENA. Is a big closet.

MRS. WYLIE. Look. I would be the first to admit that you deserve a little reward for all you've been through.

ELENA. Thanks.

MRS. WYLIE. But it's not the time!

ELENA. Okay.

MRS. WYLIE. Now first of all, I want you to get rid of the man –

ELENA. Which one?

MRS. WYLIE. ...There's more than one?

ELENA. *(Sheepishly.)* Two.

MRS. WYLIE. You've got two men in there?

ELENA. Yeah.

MRS. WYLIE. I knew you had potential, but this is incredible.

ELENA. Thanks.

MRS. WYLIE. Look I'm impressed. All right? I'm very impressed. But get them the hell out of here! Do you have any idea who's downstairs right now?

ELENA. No.

MRS. WYLIE. The police! And they're asking questions!

ELENA. *(Croaking.)* Police?

MRS. WYLIE. That's what I came up to tell you. They're looking for some madwoman who tried to break into the theatre tonight. In costume!

ELENA. Police?

> *(A knock at the front door.)*

MRS. WYLIE. Oh hell. That could be them.

> *(Lowering her voice.)*

All right. Here's the story. You're still Elena. You came back from the theatre and went straight to your room –

> *(During the following,* **MRS. WYLIE** *leads* **ELENA** *to the connecting door, to hide her in the bedroom.)*

You haven't seen anything unusual, whatsoever. And whatever we do, we keep them away from the closet!

> *(She closes the connecting door leaving* **ELENA** *in the bedroom. Another knock at the front door.)*

MRS. WYLIE. Com-ing!

(*She opens the door.* **JO** *rushes in, still dressed as Carmen.*)

JO. I've got to talk to you!

(*She closes the door.* **MRS. WYLIE** *is speechless and reels backward. Meanwhile* **ELENA**, *still in the bedroom, leans against the connecting wall, arm outstretched; and* **JO** *does the same in the sitting room. They unknowingly create a mirror image.*)

MRS. WYLIE. *This is no time for jokes, you idiot!*

JO. Jokes?

MRS. WYLIE. Are you out of your mind?! What's the matter with you?!

JO. What did *I* do?

MRS. WYLIE. This whole thing could blow up any second!

JO. I know!

MRS. WYLIE. Well who was at the door?

JO. What door?

MRS. WYLIE. That door! Who was knocking?

JO. Me.

MRS. WYLIE. Before that.

JO. How should I know?

MRS. WYLIE. You were there!

JO. Where?

MRS. WYLIE. At the door!

JO. What door?!

MRS. WYLIE. *That door!*

(Pause. They're at an impasse. At this point, **ELENA** *opens the bedroom/corridor door, and exits, pulling the door closed quietly behind her.* **MRS. WYLIE** *continues, trying to restrain herself:)*

Jo. A minute ago, you were standing here and I was talking to you. There was a knock at the door, and I said, "That may be the police –"

JO. It wasn't me.

MRS. WYLIE. I know that!

JO. I mean in here!

MRS. WYLIE. Jo –

JO. I was downstairs, looking for you! When I couldn't find you, I came back up!

MRS. WYLIE. You were looking for me?

JO. Yes!

MRS. WYLIE. Why were you looking for me?

JO. That's what I want to tell you. She's gone.

MRS. WYLIE. Who?

JO. Elena! She's gone!

MRS. WYLIE. Jo, we all have to go sometime.

JO. I mean she's not on the bed! She disappeared! Look. You told me to go change and you went downstairs. I walked in there and I tried not to look, but I couldn't help it, so I looked at the bed and she wasn't there.

MRS. WYLIE. She's in the closet.

JO. Who told you that?

MRS. WYLIE. You – ...

(She freezes. She figures it out.)

MRS. WYLIE. ...Oh my God. She's alive.

(*She bolts to the connecting door and throws it open. She looks around the bedroom and sees that it's empty.*)

She's gone.

JO. But she's alive. That's terrific!

MRS. WYLIE. You idiot! She could ruin everything!

(*A knock at the front door.* **MRS. WYLIE** *and* **JO** *freeze.* **MRS. WYLIE** *lowers her voice.*)

It's either her or the police.

JO. Oh great.

MRS. WYLIE. Whatever I say, just play along.

(**JO** *sits on the sofa as* **MRS. WYLIE** *walks to the front door and opens it. The* **BELLHOP** *enters, carrying an ice bucket, a bottle of champagne, and two glasses.*)

BELLHOP. Nightcap, anyone?

MRS. WYLIE. Oh no!

BELLHOP. Miss Firenzi! Oh, ma'am, I know how tired you must be and I won't take up much of your time, but I simply must tell you how magnificent you were tonight. You were wonderful!

JO. Thanks.

BELLHOP. I'll never forget it as long as I live.

JO. You liked it, eh?

BELLHOP. I adored every note.

JO. What exactly did you like a-best?

MRS. WYLIE. (*To* **JO**.) Not now!

BELLHOP. *(Dramatically.)* When you threw the ring at Don José at the end and cried "*Cette bague autrefois, tu me l'avais donnée, tiens!*" It was so beautiful!

MRS. WYLIE. Who the hell ordered champagne?

BELLHOP. She did.

JO. I did?

MRS. WYLIE. You did?

BELLHOP. That's what they told me downstairs.

MRS. WYLIE. Oh yes of course. I remember now.

(*To* **JO.**) The champagne.

JO. Oh yeah. I forget, eh?

BELLHOP. And guess what? It's on the house, and *I* arranged it.

MRS. WYLIE. Well, that's very lovely of you.

BELLHOP. I did it for *her*.

MRS. WYLIE. Well now you've done it, so get out.

BELLHOP. *(Ignoring* **MRS. WYLIE.***)* Is there anything else I can do for you, Miss Firenzi?

JO. I done think so. Thanks.

MRS. WYLIE. Out.

BELLHOP. If you want anything, just pick up the phone. I'm on all night.

MRS. WYLIE. Out!

BELLHOP. *(Unruffled, to* **JO.***)* I'll see you later.

(Frowns.) Goodbye, Lucy.

(She exits, closing the door.)

MRS. WYLIE. All right, now listen. Here's the plan. Number one, you change. And do it this time!

JO. Yes, ma'am.

MRS. WYLIE. I'll go find Elena and explain everything. And then, if I have to, I'll pay her off.

> (**MRS. WYLIE** *goes to the front door.*)

JO. Ma'am? Since we're not doing the *Requiem*, can I do the *Tosca*?

MRS. WYLIE. Change!

JO. Yes, ma'am.

> (**MRS. WYLIE** *exits.* **JO** *walks into the bedroom, leaving the connecting door open, and heads straight for the bathroom. She walks into the bathroom and closes the door. Pause. A cry from* **JO***, and the door swings open,* **JO** *holding the handle for dear life.* **LEO***, glistening with oil and still in his towel, yanks her back in and the door slams. A cry from* **LEO***, and the door swings open,* **LEO** *comes out panting,* **JO** *yanks him back in.*)

> (*Silence for a moment; then the closet door opens and* **JERRY** *cautiously emerges. He wears a trench coat over his underwear.*)

JERRY. *(In a whisper.)* Elena?

> (*There's a yelp from the bathroom and* **JERRY** *is startled by it. Then he realizes that she must be using the bathroom.*)

Oh. Sorry!

> (*He sighs with relief and goes into the sitting room, smiling happily. Then he notices the champagne.*)

Oh, Elena! Champagne!

(He picks up one of the champagne glasses admiringly. He notices a speck of dirt on it, tries to scratch it away. Then he picks up the other one and decides they both need washing – so he walks into the kitchenette, happily humming a popular tune. At which moment:)

*(The bathroom door crashes open and **JO** reels out, breathing heavily. **LEO** follows her out still wearing a towel.)*

LEO. Now don't go vay. I have der surprise for you und I be right back.

*(He exits into the bathroom and closes the door. **JO** catches her breath, then staggers into the sitting room, closing the connecting door behind her. **JERRY**, who's heard the door, enters from the kitchenette [without the glasses].)*

JERRY. Hello, gorgeous.

(He shrugs off the trench coat and it falls to the floor. He's still in his boxer shorts.)

We're alone at last.

*(**JO** is speechless.)*

Oh you darling. You look all tuckered out.

(She shakes her head yes.)

"Tuckered out" by the way is an American expression which means "very tired" and it comes from the Puritans who wore a bib and tucker at the end of a hard day's work in the fields, and yet –

JO. Shut up and kiss me.

(*JO* and *JERRY* *begin kissing passionately and start to make love – which is when the bedroom/corridor door opens and* **ELENA** *rushes in, closing the door quickly, but quietly. She's on the lam and breathing heavily. She runs to her suitcase, grabs it, and turns to go –*)

(*When* **LEO** *enters from the bathroom. He's in a robe. They face each other and* **LEO** *shrugs off the robe – he has his undershorts on – and he looks magnificent, his body glistening with oil, every muscle toned to perfection.*)

LEO. Well. Shall ve skin der bear togeder?

ELENA. Skin a-da bear?

LEO. Ja. Dat is Dutch expression which is coming from der first explorers who vent out to der wilderness, see der bear und said –

ELENA. Shut up and a-kiss me!

(*She pushes him onto the bed, climbs on top of him, and they start to make love.*)

JO. (*In the sitting room.*) Shall we turn off a-the lights?

LEO. (*In the bedroom.*) I am liking it mitt der lights on.

JERRY. (*In the sitting room.*) If it's all right with you.

ELENA. (*In the bedroom.*) It's a-fine a-with me!

(*Both couples go at it again. As the lights fade, music comes up: the final moments of the tenor-soprano duet "Da quel di che t'incontrai" from Donizetti's* Linda di Chamounix. *It's a love song that builds to a final cry of joy from the soprano.*)

(*The lights are out.*)

Scene Two

(Fifteen minutes later.)

(When the duet is over, the lights come up. Both couples have just finished making love; and each is unaware of the other couple in the adjoining room. The two men are in their underwear and the two women are simultaneously fixing their make-up.)

JERRY. Wow. It was even better than I thought it would be. I guess that's because you're Italian.

JO. I guess so, eh?

LEO. Dey don't call me for nuttin' der Flying Dutchman, eh?

ELENA. *(Ready to faint.)* You can say that again.

LEO. Dey don't call me for nuttin' der Flying Dutchman. Zo now I go to freshen der body. Und ven I come back I turn on both of der engines.

> *(**LEO** exits into the bathroom and closes the door. **ELENA** sways from exhaustion, about to collapse.)*

JERRY. I think we should have that champagne now. What do you think?

JO. Sure. Why not, eh?

JERRY. You pop the cork, I'll dry the glasses.

(Sexy.) Maybe it'll put us in the mood again.

JO. Could be, eh?

> *(He exits into the kitchenette. The moment he's gone, **JO** breaks into song – the "Toreador Song" from Carmen. She dances to the sofa and begins opening the champagne.)*

JO.

TOREADOR, EN GARDE!
TOREADOR, TOREADOR!
ET SONGE BIEN, OUI, SONGE EN COMBATTANT
QU'UN OEIL NOIR TE REGAAAAAARDE,
ET QUE L'AMOUR T'ATTEND,
TOREADOR, L'AMOUR L'AMOUR T'ATTEND!

(When the singing begins, **ELENA** sits up in bed and listens. As **JO** continues opening the bottle, **ELENA** gets up from the bed and goes to the connecting door. She listens; then opens the door; and as she steps into the sitting room she sees **JO** – or rather, she sees herself opening a bottle of champagne and singing. She freezes, speechless. She looks down at herself, then back at **JO**. She now realizes there's a fair possibility that she's lost her mind.)

(**ELENA** steps back into the bedroom, leaving the connecting door open. Then she runs to her suitcase, grabs it, and runs from the room, out the corridor door, closing it behind her.)

(As that door closes, the bathroom door opens and **LEO** enters the bedroom, still in his underwear, with no shirt or trousers, just boxer shorts and an undershirt. He sees that the bedroom is empty but notices that the connecting door is open. He walks to the door and sees **JO** – who is still opening the champagne – and he walks into the room just as **JERRY** enters from the kitchenette, holding the glasses.)

LEO. Der champagne!

JERRY. (Simultaneously.) All set!

(The cork pops.)

(**JO** *is speechless.*)

JERRY. *(To* **LEO.***)* What are you doing here?

LEO. I am asking myself der same of you.

JERRY. This happens to be a private party.

LEO. Ja, I agree, zo please go get yourself lost.

JERRY. Elena, tell him to leave!

JO. *(To* **LEO.***)* A-leave!

LEO. No, tell *him* dat, you gorgeous t'ing!

JERRY. Elena, what is he doing here?

JO. I-I-I-I-I –

JERRY. *(To* **LEO.***)* How long have you been here?

LEO. Half hour tops.

JERRY. That's impossible. I've been here a half hour.

LEO. Ja, I know. I vas here vhen you arrived. She said she vas getting rid of you as qvick as de possum.

JERRY. Elena. Did you know he was in there?

JO. I-I-I-I-I –

JERRY. *(Pale.)* You did.

JO. It's a-not what you t'ink, eh?

JERRY. How could you do this?! After what you said to me?

LEO. She could not help herself. I used der oil.

(*They try to corner her.*)

JERRY. You...temptress.

LEO. You znake in der meadow.

JERRY. How could you do this?!

LEO. How could she not?

JO. Hey! I gotta go now...

> *(She pushes them back onto the sofa; then, in order to buy time, throws the champagne in the air and hands the vase of flowers to **LEO**. Then she bolts away.)*

LEO. Hey!

JERRY. *(Catching the champagne.)* Hey, cut that out!

> *(They chase through the sitting room, then the bedroom.)*

LEO. *Shtop!*

JERRY. *Slow down!*

> *(**JO** is going this way and that to avoid them, as though she is doing parkour. She throws **JERRY** a lamp and **LEO** a radio.)*

> *(Then **JO** dashes into the bathroom and slams the door. Bang! The men rush the door and try to open it. Too late.)*

Ah!

LEO. It is locked.

> *(**JERRY** grabs the doorknob and rattles it violently.)*

JERRY. *Come out of there, you Mata Hari!*

LEO. You are vaisting your time. She is love 'em und leave 'em.

JERRY. Well what do we do?

LEO. You do as you please, I am putting on clothings.

JERRY. Good idea.

(JERRY glares at the bathroom door; then walks into the sitting room to retrieve his shirt and trousers. Meanwhile LEO looks around the room for his clothes – then remembers he left them in the bathroom. He walks to the bathroom door.)

LEO.   Elena. My clothes are in dere.

(No response, LEO knocks on the door.)

Elena, I need my clothes.

(No response; he sees something on the floor.)

Elena, I am holding der big brassiere und ve do der exchange.

(They do it like lightning and then the door slams shut and is locked again from the inside.)

T'ank you, Elena.

(The men get dressed in the bedroom.)

JERRY.   I wouldn't have believed it was possible. She seemed so lovely.

LEO.   She iss lovely but tricky. You have got to hand it to her.

JERRY.   I did. That's the problem.

(At this moment, the front door opens and PASQUALE enters, carrying his suitcase. He leaves the door ajar.)

PASQUALE.   One a-more chance, eh? One a-more chance and that's it!

(JERRY and LEO both hear PASQUALE and look at each other, puzzled. LEO enters the sitting room.)

LEO. Oh mein Gott, she has got an udder vone!

(**PASQUALE** *is startled; then glares suspiciously at* **LEO**.)

PASQUALE. Who are you?

LEO. A friend of der family. Who are you?

PASQUALE. The family.

LEO. Elena's husband?

PASQUALE. That's a-right.

LEO. (*Calling to* **JERRY**.) Hey Romeo. Guess who's here?

PASQUALE. I'm gonna keel 'er.

(**JERRY** *enters the sitting room.*)

LEO. Ve know how you feel.

PASQUALE. You again.

LEO. You have met before?

JERRY. Just once, in the closet.

LEO. You realize dat he is Elena's husband.

JERRY. Oh sure. Only he isn't really her husband. Elena told me. He likes to pretend he is, and she plays along because she doesn't want to hurt his feelings.

PASQUALE. Elena tell you this?

JERRY. Of course she did. We made love.

PASQUALE. I'm gonna keel her. I swear before God, on everything that's a-holy, I'm gonna strangle her!

LEO. Und yet he sounds like her husband.

PASQUALE. With my bare hands!

LEO. He's her husband.

JERRY. But she said...

> (*He realizes.*)

Oh my God.

PASQUALE. Where is she?

> (**JERRY** *and* **LEO** *look at each other.*)

Where is she?!

JERRY & LEO. The bathroom.

> (**PASQUALE** *stalks into the bedroom, toward the bathroom door.* **LEO** *and* **JERRY** *follow him.*)

LEO. She lock herself in.

JERRY. She won't come out.

LEO. Ve tried!

JERRY. You're sure you're her husband?

> (**PASQUALE** *growls in response, which scares them both. Then he tries the door, without success.*)

PASQUALE. Elena. I's a-Pasquale.

JO. (*Offstage.*) Oh no!

PASQUALE. (*Banging on the door with his fist.*) Open the door right now, 'cause if that is you in there, I'm a-callin' the Pope!

> (*As* **PASQUALE** *bangs and hollers, there's an eruption of overlapping voices as* **ELENA** *runs in through the front door pursued by* **MRS. WYLIE, JULIA,** *and the* **BELLHOP.**)

ELENA. Help!

MRS. WYLIE. Stop!

JULIA. Elena! Please!

ELENA. Help!

BELLHOP. Leave her alone!

ELENA. Help!

MRS. WYLIE. I just want to talk to you!

JULIA. Elena, you promised!

> (**PASQUALE, LEO,** *and* **JERRY** *have by now
> entered the sitting room to see what's going on.*)

PASQUALE. Elena!

ELENA. Pasquale!

> *(She runs to him.)*

Oh, Pasquale! Get me outa here! Please!

PASQUALE. *(Wheeling on* **LEO** *and* **JERRY**.*)* So! You make a-fun of me, eh? You tell a-me lies!

MRS. WYLIE. What are you two doing here?

JERRY. Well...

LEO. Ve are passing by, zo ve are shtopping in.

JERRY. To get her autograph.

BELLHOP. Did you get it?!

JERRY. We sure did.

PASQUALE. *(To* **ELENA**.*)* They told a-me you were locked in the bathroom.

JULIA. The bathroom?

PASQUALE. They make a-me think you were fooling around!

ELENA. Pasquale? Me?

JERRY. We didn't say that.

LEO. No dat is silly.

JERRY. We were waiting

LEO. here in der room

JERRY. when somebody rushes in there,

LEO. zoom, she goes by,

JERRY. who sort of looked like Elena,

LEO. she had der face,

JERRY. and the body,

LEO. but vas different person,

JERRY. entirely!

JULIA. Oh my God. It's the lunatic! It must be!

PASQUALE. Luna-what!

JULIA. Lunatic. A madwoman. She's running around the city pretending she's your wife. And apparently she's violent. She actually hit a policeman!

ELENA. No!

JULIA. Yes! We should call the police.

MRS. WYLIE. Julia, please.

JULIA. But she could be dangerous, Lucy!

MRS. WYLIE. Oh I doubt that very much.

BELLHOP. Let's see who it is!

MRS. WYLIE. Stay out of this!

PASQUALE. She's a-right, eh? I wanna see this a-lunatic. Pasquale want to see her!

(He walks into the bedroom, followed by the others, who speak simultaneously.)

MRS. WYLIE. Oh I wouldn't bother –

LEO. It is in der past –

JERRY. Who cares who it is?!

BELLHOP. But I want to see her!

PASQUALE. *(At the bathroom door; hollering.)* Hello?! Who's in there?

> *(No response.* **PASQUALE** *bangs on the door.)*

Come outa there! You hear me?!

BELLHOP. This-is-the-police! Come-out-with-your-hands-up!

> *(They all look at her. She looks behind herself and shrugs.)*

PASQUALE. I'm gonna give you three numbers! One! …Two!

> *(The door unlocks…then opens…and* **JO** *emerges, herself again. Her wig is off, no make-up, no costume. And she wears her party dress for the big night.)*

JO. Did I miss something?

BELLHOP. It's Jo.

JERRY. *(Shocked, sitting down on the bed.)* Jo?

MRS. WYLIE. Jo! What a surprise!

PASQUALE. She doesn't even look a-like Elena!

JO. Hi, Elena! You look great!

ELENA. Jo! My friend! They drive a-me crazy. You done know!

JO. Gee, I'm sorry.

ELENA. Pasquale, please! Take a-me home! We start again and make a-happy marriage.

PASQUALE. That's just what I'm a-thinkin'.

ELENA. Carissimo

PASQUALE. Bellezza.

ELENA. Mia vongole.

PASQUALE. Let's go!

>   (*They head for the door.*)

> (*To* **ELENA.**) We go to Greece, eh?

ELENA. Greece. That's a-good. I take a rest.

JULIA. Elena, you promised!

BELLHOP. My autograph!

PASQUALE. *Leave her alone!*

JULIA, MRS. WYLIE & BELLHOP. Right!

>   (**JULIA, MRS. WYLIE,** *and the* **BELLHOP** *retreat
>   into the sitting room followed by* **PASQUALE**
>   *and* **LEO.**)

JO. Bye, Elena.

ELENA. Jo. Thanks a-for everything, eh?

JO. Take care of yourself.

ELENA. And done forget. You gotta say I'm a-the best. I'm
a-Jo.

JO & ELENA. (*Together.*) I sing good!

PASQUALE. (*At the sitting room/corridor door.*) Elena!
Let's a-go!

ELENA. Pasquale. My love.

>   (**ELENA** *joins* **PASQUALE** *at the door and they
>   exit.*)

JULIA. Wait!

(**JULIA** *hurries to the door.*)

JULIA. Just five minutes, that's all I need!

(*She exits, running.*)

Elena! Please!

(*Pause.*)

MRS. WYLIE. Well…I guess that's that. Everything seems to be in order now.

(**JO** *and* **JERRY** *are next to each other. He looks at her in confusion, realizing now that he slept with her.*)

JO. Yeah.

LEO. Tip a top.

JERRY. Just fine.

(**MRS. WYLIE** *eyes* **JERRY** *with suspicion.*)

Is anything wrong?

MRS. WYLIE. I'll speak to you later, young man. You don't think I believe that story about the autograph, do you?

(*The* **BELLHOP** *has by now picked up a piece of paper from the coffee table.*)

BELLHOP. (*Reading.*) "To Jerry. A very special person, and handsome to look at. Firenzi."

MRS. WYLIE. (*Snatching the paper.*) Let me see that!

BELLHOP. I wish I'd gotten one.

JO. You still might catch her.

BELLHOP. Do you think so?!

JO. It's worth a try.

(The **BELLHOP** *bolts out of the room and down the corridor.)*

BELLHOP. *(As she exits.)* Miss Firenzi! Miss Firenzi!

JERRY. *(Taking his autograph from* **MRS. WYLIE.***)* I'll take that, thank you.

MRS. WYLIE. *(Puzzled.)* Yes, of course.

(During the following **JERRY** *stares at the paper, lost in thought.)*

LEO. Lucy, is dat party of yours downstairs still voopin'?

MRS. WYLIE. I think so.

LEO. Good. Ve dance, ve nibble, who knows vhat happens. And den I take you to a supper club.

MRS. WYLIE. Dutch treat?

LEO. Ja, dat's vhat dey call me. Ha!

(He takes **MRS. WYLIE***'s arm and she beams. They head for the door.)*

JO. Ma'am? Shall we say tomorrow morning? Ten o'clock. Your office.

MRS. WYLIE. Jo –

JO. You see, I've got some new ideas for next season –

MRS. WYLIE. Jo!

JO. *Tosca, La Bohème.* Then finish off with something lighter –

MRS. WYLIE. Like *Die Fledermaus*?

JO. Good idea.

MRS. WYLIE. I'll see you in the morning, Jo. My office, ten-thirty.

JO. Ma'am.

MRS. WYLIE. Jo?

JO. Don't be late.

> (**MRS. WYLIE** *reacts and exits.* **LEO** *pauses in the doorway, gives* **JO** *a "thumbs up," then follows* **MRS. WYLIE**, *closing the door behind them.* **JO** *and* **JERRY** *are alone.*)

JERRY. Well...at least I had a fling.

JO. Yeah.

JERRY. Jo. I...I really liked it.

JO. Me too.

JERRY. And I'm glad it was with you.

JO. Me too.

JERRY. But you really took an awful chance, you know, wearing her costume, the fuss at the stage door. And hitting a policeman! If you hadn't gotten away, you might be in prison!

JO. Jerry –

JERRY. The worst part is, you didn't get to hear her sing. And she was so terrific.

JO. Was she?

JERRY. Oh, Jo, she was unbelievable. When she first came out, a...a shock went through the audience. And then she sang and... I know it sounds silly, but I started to...

JO. Cry?

JERRY. Yeah. I couldn't help it. I guess that's why she's Elena Firenzi.

JO. Could be.

> (*Music begins playing: the final moments of the Habanera from Act I of* Carmen. **JO** *hears it;* **JERRY** *doesn't.*)

JERRY. And even then I was thinking, dammit, where's Jo? I want *her* to hear this. I want to share it with her.

> (**JO** *takes* **JERRY**'s *hand and puts it to her cheek.* **JERRY** *still doesn't get it, but is lulled by her voice and closes his eyes.*)

JO. *(Singing.)*
L'AMOUR EST ENFANT DE BOHÈME,
IL N'A JAMAIS CONNU DE LOI,
SI TU NE M'AIMES PAS, JE T'AIME;
SI JE T'AIME, PRENDS GARDE À TOI!

> (*As* **JO** *holds the final note,* **JERRY**'s *eyes snap open and his jaw drops. He realizes at last.*)

JERRY. Jo!

> (*They kiss each other like there's no tomorrow.*)

> (*Fireworks go off all over the place through the final swell as...*)

> (*The curtain falls.*)

CURTAIN CALL

In the original Alley Theatre production, the play proper was followed by an elaborate curtain call of sorts – that is, the actors pantomimed the entire action of the play in eighty-five seconds to the music of the Finale to Jacques Ibert's *Divertissement*. (*Divertissement* was written by Ibert in 1930 as incidental music for Labiche's farce, *Un Chapeau de Paille d'Italie*. The music is therefore not only the right length but also superbly frantic. It's also generally available.)

A scenario describing the action of the curtain call is set forth below. The action is divided into numbered paragraphs for the sake of convenience in rehearsal. However, the action is intended to flow continuously from beginning to end without a pause, with the actors literally running from one place to the next where necessary. It's also essential that the actors use extremely broad gestures so that the story emerges as clearly (and frantically) as possible.

To avoid confusion, it should be noted that in some instances, entrances and exits occur through different doors than they do in the play proper and that, in condensing the story to eighty-five seconds, some portions of the action have been consciously omitted. A few props may have to be pre-set before the curtain call can begin. However, the curtain call should explode into action as soon as possible after the play is ended.

The director should feel free to change the action of the curtain call, where necessary, to reflect any business that may have been added to the particular production. For example, the director should choose a costume piece which quickly and clearly establishes the Carmen costume. The Carmen head piece is suggested here, but that may not work for every production.

Finally, it is important to make the curtain call feel dangerous. It must never look easy. Even when the cast has rehearsed it so well that they can do it in their sleep, it must always appear to the audience that it's a tour de force of speed and ingenuity and that tonight may be the night that the cast can't pull it off. I have seen many theater companies take so much pride in how well they've learned the curtain call that they purposely make it look easy. That's absolutely the wrong approach. Strive for the opposite. Make it look as difficult, breakneck, breathless, and dangerous as possible. It should end exactly on the last note of music because the audience should feel that the cast barely got there in time. It's a performance, and, like all performances, it should feel that this night of all nights it was special and a tremendous accomplishment.

P.S.: Always play the music at full volume so that the whole thing feels as exuberant and exciting as possible.

SCENARIO

1. **JO** and **JERRY** are onstage in the sitting room. **JERRY**, on the pouf, swoons with pleasure (thereby cueing the start of the music). **JO** answers the phone and reacts to **MRS. WYLIE**'s yell; and **MRS. WYLIE** walks in from the corridor.

2. **MRS. WYLIE** points at **JERRY**, then at the door (telling him to leave). **JERRY** walks through the connecting door and straight into the closet.

3. **JO** and **MRS. WYLIE** hear the phone. **JO** answers it, indicates that it's **ELENA**, and hangs up. **MRS. WYLIE** opens the sitting room/corridor door and the **FIRENZIS** walk in. **ELENA** of course is still dressed as Carmen from the end of the play, but she has her fur stole over her shoulders at the moment.

4. **ELENA** and **PASQUALE** sling their coat/fur stole at **JO**, as the **BELLHOP** enters the bedroom from the corridor and throws her arms up, singing.

5. **JO** hands the coat and fur stole to the **BELLHOP** at the connecting door. The **BELLHOP** opens the closet door and throws the coat and stole in to **JERRY**. Then she exits into the corridor.

6. Meanwhile, **ELENA** and **PASQUALE** argue. Then **PASQUALE** stalks into the bedroom and straight into the bathroom, slamming the door.

7. **MRS. WYLIE** picks up the phone and screams. She slams down the phone and walks out.

8. **ELENA** and **JO** "shake" themselves, then sing, arms out. Then each picks up a wine glass and stirs the other's drink with her finger.

9. **PASQUALE** emerges from the bathroom, making his farewell gesture. Then he walks to the closet, opens the door, sees **JERRY** and stifles a growl. **PASQUALE** stalks out into the corridor, followed by **JERRY**.

10. **ELENA** staggers into the bedroom, picks up the farewell note, screams and collapses onto the bed. **JO** heads for the bedroom. As she passes the corridor door, **LEO** enters, gives **JO** a kiss and exits. Then **JO** enters the bedroom as **MRS. WYLIE** enters the bedroom from the corridor.

11. **JO** points at **ELENA** ("She's dead!") and **MRS. WYLIE** climbs onto the bed and starts shaking the corpse. **MRS. WYLIE** then pulls the Carmen head piece from a hidden spot (perhaps the night table), throws it at **JO** and points to the bathroom.

12. **JO** reacts with horror, then exits into the bathroom, as **MRS. WYLIE** walks to the sitting room/corridor door and opens it. **JULIA** and the **BELLHOP** enter. **MRS. WYLIE** grabs the **BELLHOP** by the lapels and **JERRY** rushes into the sitting room from the corridor, holding the rose.

13. **MRS. WYLIE, JERRY, JULIA**, and the **BELLHOP** chase around the sofa, halt for the **BELLHOP**'s flash picture, then continue the chase, as **JO** enters (in the Carmen head piece) from the bathroom. She walks to the upstage "wall" dividing the two rooms. Looks at the audience and shrugs, then steps through the wall.

14. **JERRY** hands **JO** the rose. She indicates that she'll do the opera, and everyone (except **JO**) registers elation.

15. Everyone in the sitting room exits into the corridor, as **ELENA** gets up from the bed. She runs into the sitting room and sits on the sofa. Simultaneously, **JO** enters the bedroom from the corridor, discovers that **ELENA**'s gone and runs back out the same door.

16. **JULIA** runs into the sitting room from the corridor and frightens **ELENA**. She ushers her back out into the corridor, then walks into the bedroom – as **JO** enters the sitting room from the corridor.

17. Immediately, **JERRY** enters the sitting room from the kitchenette and **LEO** enters the bedroom from the bathroom. The **WOMEN** push them onto the sofa and bed, respectively.

18. **JERRY** goes back into the kitchenette and **LEO** stands back to allow **ELENA** to find to her feet. As **JO** picks up the champagne, **ELENA** enters the sitting room, sees **JO**, reacts, puts the champagne down, then runs out the sitting room/corridor door.

19. **LEO**, hard on **ELENA**'s heels, enters the sitting room as **JERRY** reenters the sitting room from the kitchenette. They both discover **JO** at the same time, and all three react.

20. **JERRY** and **LEO** chase **JO** through the bedroom to the bathroom door. **JO** exits into the bathroom, closing the door before they can catch her. As soon as **JO** slams the door, **PASQUALE** enters the bedroom from the corridor.

21. **JERRY** and **LEO** point to the bathroom. **PASQUALE** bangs on the door as **ELENA, MRS. WYLIE, JULIA**, and the **BELLHOP** run into the sitting room and then into the bedroom, where they see the three men and stop.

22. **PASQUALE** hits the bathroom door again, and **JO** strolls out of the bathroom (without her Carmen head piece). She gestures "What's the matter?" Shock from the others.

23. Everyone exits except **JO** and **JERRY**: **PASQUALE, ELENA**, and **MRS. WYLIE** go through the sitting room and out the sitting room/corridor door, as **JULIA**, the **BELLHOP**, and **LEO** exit through the bedroom/corridor door. **JO** and **JERRY** simultaneously walk into the sitting room.

24. **JO** throws her arms up, singing. **JERRY** cries "Jo!" and they kiss. Blackout.

(Traditional curtain calls now follow.)